CONFESSIONS OF A VILLAIN

NOA

Cover by: Petrija Pajic
Edited by: Shel Sweeney
Editor's Company: A Worded Life
Production Assistant: Power of Words. www.powerofwords.com.au

ISBN-10: 0-646-95363-X
ISBN-13: 978-0-646-95363-2
Cataloguing-in-Publication data: Creator: NOA, author.
Title: Confessions of a villain / NOA.
Subjects: Autobiographical fiction, Australian.
Dewey Number: A823.4

Website: www.noasworld.com
Social Media Pages: www.facebook.com/NOAmusician
www.youtube.com/NOAmusician
Instagram and Snapchat: @noaofficial
NOA would love your feedback on the book at your retailer or any of the listed social media.

Printed in Australia

"God's effectuation is not supported by what we want. It is a delivery of what we need. What we do with this bestowal of his grace is our own choice."

Dedication

To my sister,
Who I am born to protect
To my mother,
Who I will always love
To my family and friends,
Whom I owe everything
To any star that wishes to shine,
Who I will always fight for

Contents

Author's Note

This piece of writing is a fictional autobiography. Names, characters, businesses, places, events and incidents are either the products of my imagination or have been written as a twisted version of a reality that may or may not have ever existed. Any resemblance to actual events or actual persons, living or dead, are categorically coincidental or substitutional.

I have fabricated many events, locales and conversations from certain memories I hold; some of these memories are an unobstructed description of my truth, while other memories, over time, have become fractured. Memory holds inevitable flaws, which is why imagination is needed to piece things together. There are several parallels to reality that one may find throughout the progression of this story, however, any comparisons that may be deduced by the reader should be considered as serendipitous.

This story is my own personal recollection of events that may or may not have ever occurred. Individuals perceive things in many different ways and what I feel to be my own truth, another might dispute.

And with this information, I deeply hope that you enjoy this fictive recollection and invention of my life.

Prologue

I fear humanity's progress.

We are taught to lie, selfishly, to get ahead.

I fear mistrust.

If we can blatantly lie to our lovers, then to whom can we be truly honest?

I fear decisions.

To arbitrate right and wrong means, that as humans, there is an error that we are capable of choosing.

I fear love.

For love is one thing that we intrinsically desire, which brings us so much horror.

I fear success.

We are never happy with what we have; we replace our achievements with more goals.

I fear the eyes of the world.

Others judge us the moment we step out into any place where humans reside.

I fear talent.

Possessing something brings others wishing to steal what you own.

Actually, now that I think about it, I don't fear at all.

Chapter One

The Furtive Move Before the Storm

Villainy is criminal behaviour, and while I wouldn't call myself a criminal, my behaviour has, nonetheless, always been somewhat wicked. Don't get me wrong, I am not condoning wickedness or evil, but I do believe everyone should at least have a little bit of an egregiously disobedient streak in them. Life would be pretty boring if you were hushed and diplomatic all the time...'Yes, sir, no, sir, three bags full, sir'. Sometimes, it's important to transgress the rules, to be shameless and outrageous. In short, to be a badass, and if lying to your mother in order to go to an audition is badass, then I'm proud to hold that title!

*

The night prior to the day that changed my life, the television was tuned into the news. Ellis Degencourt, a famous comedian from the US, was on her way to the land down under to film an episode of her TV talk show in Sydney. The hype was phenomenal. Though she had never been to Australia before, the majority of the country loved to watch her hilarious program.

My family and I were excitedly scrutinising the news segment about Ellis' impending arrival when an ad break overrode the newscast.

> *It's that time of the year again, Australia! Head down to Milestone Arena this Sunday to audition for the latest season of 'Star Power'. Who knows? You could be Australia's next Star Power Winner this coming 2013! General admission closes at 5pm, so get down there early to warm up your voices and try your luck at becoming Australia's next Star Power!*

Normally I would have ignored these types of ads like I had numerous times before, but this time something stirred inside me. It bubbled and churned within like a witch's cauldron and, just like that, I was caught in a moment of possibility. The label I was signed to, Teddy Productions, had stopped encouraging my musical decisions and wasn't stimulating my creativity anymore. I had already been with them for over three years and my contract didn't define or lock me in for any authorised period of time. I guess I was feeling a little stifled, limited, held back. I wouldn't say the label was underfunded, but to produce, promote and escalate the career of a pop star you need a lot of financing and Teddy Productions just didn't seem to have the resources. In the three years since I first signed with them, I had only released one song (over the Internet) while hundreds of recordings and masters sat on a hard drive in a studio—unheard.

Every month, Teddy Productions held local performances at the bar across the road from the label's studios. This bar only had a capacity to hold fifty people and it was the exact same people each month. They came to drink beer and, for the most part, ignore whatever else was going on around them. I wouldn't have exactly called these gigs an opportunity, but that's where my manager at the time, Ted, decided I should perform.

Don't get me wrong, I admired Ted like I would have a big brother. Ted was a really passionate and loving person. He was a real life teddy bear with a passion for music and a heart of gold... like the gold he thought he saw in his future when he looked at me. That's all I will ever be to a label: a symbol of potential cash or economic deprivation. As an artist you're either going to make money for your label and manager, or you're going to flunk. But that is the risk a label takes! Your label should benevolently provide you with opportunities to reach your potential, to get you to that point where you can make that cash for them... but with Teddy Productions, this wasn't happening. Ted was a suit and tie kind of guy, a business man. He also managed a law firm and was very intelligent. He demonstrated his aptitude for management by manipulating producers and dancers into working free of charge. I remember him saying, "You have to coax them into doing what you want them to do. Make them feel special and valued. That way, they'll always come back. They'll come to rehearsals; they'll commit."

It was only after I left the label that I realised that Ted was using his intelligence to apply this method to me too! I really loved Ted and his whole family, but sometimes you just have to remember that your family only really consists of those with the same blood running through their veins as you. Of course there are always those close friends you consider family too, but here's the thing... there are only a small number of people, a marginalised faction of those, who do not share that blood-bond with you of whom you do have to be very cautious.

The next ad came on the television screen and I crept into my room with my phone clenched in my fist. Mum was making dinner and my sister Christine was in her room, as usual, probably texting her boyfriend. I dialled my best friend Drita's number and sat at the edge of my bed staring at the singing and dancing trophies on the top shelf of my desk. Scanning across, I could see all the awards and medals I had won – proof of the talent I know I had.

Unfortunately, sometimes there are people who don't get the opportunity to prove or demonstrate their own talents. I'm not one of those people to let opportunity slip by. I know I have talent.

"Ye," Drita answered, as she chewed on mouthfuls of Serbian salami in a way that could be heard from a suburb away.

"Hey, it's me. Can you do me a favour... pretty... please?" I panhandled, using my Stitch voice from Disney's 'Lilo and Stitch'. In my experience, you always get a positive answer when a Stitch voice is used.

"What now loser?" Drita asked in vex, she probably knew this was going to be some type of overbearing request to go to a strange and far away shopping centre on one of my crusades again.

"Well... I wanna audition for the show."

"Huh? What show?"

"Star Power. The one on TV... Haven't you seen the ads?"

"Umm... Aren't you signed already? Are you even allowed to audition?" she asked. I could tell from her interrogative tone that she was curious, but Drita is, and be, always overprotective of me. She doesn't like it when I get into sticky situations, especially with her in tow, but she supports me every time nonetheless.

"Yeah, Dreets. I know this is kind of random, but... I don't know... I just saw the ad on TV and I... well, I just have to go. You know I've wanted to be on a show like this since 'Popstar Idol' came out and I'm just over all this shit with Ted. I can't do it anymore. I want to feel like I'm getting somewhere. I want to be acknowledged. Like seriously..."

This was true. I remember being really young and watching all these singing competitions on television, dreaming that I would one day follow in my favourite artists' footsteps and win a show, become super famous and get out of the hole I called my life. Something was drawing me to go.

"Calm down, mate. We'll go if that's what you want, but don't expect too much from those shows. You know how it is..." she paused, "I don't even know why you're going anyways, you always said they were rigged, so why would you go?"

This was true, but being on television when I was younger had made me hope that this show wasn't as rigged as what I thought it might be. What was the worst that could happen? I would completely fail on national television? Well, I knew that just wasn't an option. So what was I afraid of? That the head music managers who run everything would choose a different winner? I wouldn't even have a chance of winning if I didn't at least try!

I used to ponder aimlessly and constantly about who ran the music industry. Who were these managers? Were they the Illuminati? Were they simply random, heartless business people placed in charge of major record companies, in for the money and nothing else? Were they failed musicians jealous of the talent of others? I had no clue. No idea. I just had this unshakeable feeling that there was something bigger than music going on. I remember thinking: *Whoever these sharks are, if only they could just see me somehow, then I would convince them that I am worth noticing, worthy of their investment. That would be great. Would I have to sell my soul for fame? Who cares! At least I would be in on all their secrets.*

"I just have to go, Dreets. Something is telling me that I need to go," I responded.

She sighed. "What time?"

"Umm..." I smiled to myself knowing all along that she would go with me, that she had my back yet again. "I'll get my mum to drop us off at the train station at around 6. "Is that okay?"

"6pm?"

"Ah... 6am!"

"Oh, God! LOL, seriously?"

"Yeah, I'm telling her we're going to see Ellis."

"Ellis Degencourt, the comedian?"

"Yeah, she's filming at the same arena tomorrow too."

"Ajme[1], tomorrow's going to be a disaster... but if you want to go earlier, we can. I know it means a lot to you... I don't mind."

---

1 Slavic word for: God help me

"Thanks, Drita! I guess we'll just have to see, hey? I'll text you later. Thanks, times a hundred! Love ya!" I hung up.

After texting Drita the details for the next day, I went to ask Mum for a lift in the morning. Walking out of my room, my eyes flicked to my CD collection. I'm the type of artist who supports other artists. From a young age, I always bought CDs and merchandise, and still to this day I love placing a CD into my Discman to listen to tracks in a more authentic way, listening to a whole album rather than just playing a single track through a Smartphone or iPod. Flicking through the CDs, I pulled out the album by the previous year's Star Power winner, Serenity Hayes. I fiddled with the case, running my fingers over the album title. Now it was my time to shine!

Mum was in the kitchen, on the phone to my Dad. She was yelling at him to come home; the usual. I waited until she finished and started to cut some vegetables for dinner.

"Mum, can you please drop me and Drita off in the morning to the station at 6am? We're going to see Ellis in the city, to try and get seats for the taping of her show here." I knew how Mum liked to be asked things. I asked with all the right correctness, including all the information she would need to make a decision. If Mum said no, Mum meant no. To ask for a favour from Mum meant giving her all the information upfront so that she could assess and the situation and calculate the best way she could annoy me by asking questions and demanding even more information, before giving me a final yes or no answer.

"Who else is going?" she questioned.

"Umm... Just me and Drita, and maybe Maja."

"Until what time?"

"I'm not sure what time it will finish exactly, but roughly around 5pm... You know how delayed things are when filming."

"How are you getting home?" She placed her hands on her hips, still clutching the knife she was using to cut the vegetables. Another question.

"Drita's mum is going to bring us home."

She ran her fingers through her unkempt hair, oily from a hard day's work at the takeaway shop. I could see her thinking about her response. Finally she gave me the usual, one word answer.

"Fine."

*

My shower that morning was awfully quick (and I don't have short showers... ever). I began getting ready for the auditions with Drita, looking down at my favourite outfit sprawled upon my bed. I would literally be dressed in designer, Jeremy Scott, from head to toe. I had his Teddy Bear sneakers on, which had huge, plush, teddy bear heads at the base of my toes, paired with his Adidas sports jacket, which had awesome tuxedo tails trailing to the floor. Coupled with these were Jeremy's leopard and gold cheetah print pants, along with chunks of gold bracelets and neck chains. Nobody would be wearing anything like my outfit!

After picking up Drita, we headed to the train station where Mum dropped us off, before making our way to the city. From the city station we caught a cab to the arena where the auditions were being held. Luckily we arrived early at about a quarter to eight, as ten minutes after we arrived the arena was packed with a multitude of hopeful performers. Thousands upon thousands were there to audition to be the next Australian megastar. Glancing around the crowd, I didn't see anyone else who looked like me. In my world, having a unique look is a good thing... a great thing!

As we queued up in the line that spiralled around the large oval-shaped arena, my friend, Maja, also came to join us. She was beginning work in the city a few hours later and came by beforehand to give me a morale boost. The support of my two close friends was all that I needed. Part of me wished my sister or my Mum had come with me, but something inside was telling me that I needed to do this on my own.

All the hopeful competitors waiting to audition were given Star Power stickers with a number. My number was 4927. Over forty-nine thousand people had already auditioned or would audition before me! This was an outrageous number! What were the chances that I was going to be chosen? Slim to none! As the minutes raced by, nerves caught up with me. A man with an earpiece strapped to his ear called out numbers chronologically, and ushered each performer to enter one of the five audition rooms.

The five audition rooms were in operation at the same time. This wasn't how the television show had shown the auditions to be in the past. In previous years, it had seemed like the contestants had auditioned and performed in a large arena stage performance, with thousands of spectators there, joined by a team of celebrity judges who made their verdict. Clearly I was mistaken.

I headed to a nearby bathroom to wash away the nerves before my number was called and bumped into a short, petite girl holding a guitar. She looked (in all honesty) like any other typical female singer: tanned, pretty face, sexy physique, perfectly styled as the archetypal, pop-diva lookalike. What caught my eye though was not her beauty (I didn't have time for that), but a yellow piece of cardboard that waved in her hand as she walked past. On this piece of paper were two black letters reading: 'SP'. I wondered what this was and nicely asked her, in case I was missing out on some important paperwork. We had been asked to sign release documents and confidentiality agreements when we received our audition numbers: 'standard protocol for television programs,' we were told. No broadcast channel wants its 'secrets' to get out.

"No, you haven't missed anything, I've just gotten into the next round of auditions upstairs and this is the paper you get to move on. My name's Belle, by the way, you?" she grinned, blissfully, a jubilant smile that showed her white teeth and lit up her face.

"Hey, I'm NOA. Thanks for letting me know, I always get freaked out that I haven't done something correctly... So what happens in there?" I asked. It's always good to ask someone who has gone in first for a run down before entering an audition room yourself. It's a great heads up.

"Umm, nothing major. You sing, they write down some notes about you and send you upstairs. I think this is just how they filter out people before you actually audition for the producers of the show."

"Producers, what do you mean?" I was confused. What the hell she was talking about? *Filtering* people out? What did that mean? My face dropped completely, in shock, and my mind raced to calculate what was going on. More importantly who were these 'producers' and what did you have to do to impress them? At least with the celebrity judges you know what you're in for. Would these producers be in suits, on a panel waiting to judge us too?

"Honey, the *real* auditions aren't on today. You have to get through to the producers. They're the ones who decide if you get to audition in front of the judges."

"Oh..." I was clearly surprised.

"You didn't know?"

"No. I had assumed there would be a couple of rounds beforehand, but I still thought the celebrity judges saw us today..." That was a lie. I had no idea there would be a couple of rounds at all. But I guess that made sense. Famous people don't want to waste their whole day sitting through torturous, ear-wrenching songs.

"Well, I've auditioned a few times and have never made it through, so I'm excited that I'm going upstairs. You look pretty funky anyway, here's my number if you ever have any questions or if you get through too! I occasionally sing back up for Serenity Hayes, so I'll have all the details about the process after this."

What? She was a back-up singer for Serenity Hayes! Serenity Hayes, the show's winner from the previous year! Belle said she had tried out for three years and had never gotten past these 'filter rounds'. What chance did I have? Back-up singers usually carry the lead vocals and have to be ten times better than the singer who's singing the lead. Of course, this wasn't anything the public was aware of.

Panic struck… I could feel it rising in my chest. Breathe! I had everything to gain from this experience. I remember thinking: *If I fail, I won't have missed anything… but likewise, I won't have gained anything either.*

I had just left my label and had no source of funding and no one to help me, and in this game, you always have to be on an upward incline.

Never plateau, always rise.

Never decline, always provide.

Belle and I exchanged numbers and as I walked away I remembered the proverb Mr Myers (the Director of Kitty Kat Sundays) always said to me and the other Kitty Kat kids. He basically meant that, as performers, we should never halt in our progress, we should never stand still or stop growing, we should always provide the audience with entertainment, always improving and never lowering our skill levels. The auditions for Kitty Kat Sundays were nothing like the one I was about to experience.

I had always been talented, even as a young kid. Singing on my grandparents' backyard swing was my favourite pastime. Discman in hand, I remember swinging and singing to Rihanna, Beyoncé, Britney Spears and The Spice Girls. The school choir was my domain and plastic echo microphones were a necessity back then. That's why, when the opportunity arose to enter a local singing competition, my mother gladly gave me permission. Notice I said my mother, I didn't say my father.

My grandparents lived in Roseville and the Kitty Kat Sundays competition was a kind of 'talent search' for upcoming talent in the area. Auditions were held every consecutive Sunday for six weeks until the semi-finalists were announced. After that, another two weeks were allocated to the semi-finals and the following week the grand final was to be held. What was exciting about these auditions was that, as an eight year old, I was unable to understand what nerves really were. As an eight year old, you don't have a fear of judgement or failure. At that age, it's all fun and you just go for it with no regrets; I mean, do you even know what regret is at eight?

What made winning this competition such a great opportunity was that the top eight contestants were to be selected to appear and feature on Kitty Kat Sundays, a TV program for kids, that was nationally broadcast every Sunday for the season. This meant three months of face-time on TV and, for a child like me, this would be a major achievement.

My audition process in Roseville began with me singing the famous movie hit: 'Hakuna Matata' from the Disney movie 'The Lion King'. Walt Disney is known all over the world for his cartoons and cartoon feature films. I always loved his movies and still love them to this day. My favourite, naturally, being 'The Lion King.

I wore a lion's mask and a cute matching tan tracksuit. (Yes, I was rocking matching tracksuits in the nineties! Still chic to this day!) I roared on the stage and sang my heart out. Not to be biased, but I was a cute kid. I mean most Eurasian kids are cute. I was ethnic looking with brown hair, brown eyes, big eyelashes and a proportionate build. I had perfectly oval-shaped eyes, fair skin and a good complexion. Who wouldn't want that in a kid?

After successfully getting through the first rounds, I proceeded to the finals, I sang the same song and was selected to be one of the eight children to be on the show. It was a huge opportunity for me, and the managers of the competition event were incredibly lovely and caring.

I hold the experience fondly in my mind. I remember riding in limousines and attending red carpet premieres of Kitty Kat on Ice and Kitty Kat movies. I recall taking my mum, sister and cousin, Ellen, to one of these premieres. They had to stand on the other side of the red, velvet rope whilst myself and the other kids on the show rode up and got out of a limousine ready for press interviews. Not to say that I was happy that my family were on the other side of the rope, but I loved the sense of exceptional circumstance I had surrounding my life at that time: the sense of individuality that no 'normal' kid possessed. At such a young age, I was already my own person with my own life, dreams and choices.

I remember the children who didn't make it through to be on the show. They were rewarded with a novelty prize, a hug and a huge speech that explained to them something like 'never give up' and 'hold your head up high'. No, they didn't receive the same luxury as the final eight, but it was a good lesson for kids to learn, to show them that sometimes life isn't fair, but that you always have decent people to guide you and to comfort you.

I had a feeling that being comforted wasn't going to be the case on the morning of the Star Power auditions. I didn't think any 'filter decider' or producer was going to comfort me at all. I was no longer eight years old and this was no Kitty Kat Sunday!

After I returned from my trip to the bathroom to Drita and Maja, we waited another three hours before my number was called. The other contestants and I were like a pack of cattle walking into the slaughterhouse. What we were unaware of at that time was that afterwards, out of a group of ten, two would walk out crying, one would completely rage in fit and one other would get a yellow ticket. This meant that only one out of ten would get through, and this is what I call 'filtering'.

Before following the procession further, I kissed Maja goodbye; she was leaving for work and went in for a comfort hug from Drita. As Drita would say 'comfort is for sissies' so Maja tapped me on the shoulder instead and said, 'Good luck, mate! Ya' gonna get in ya star.' She mimicked a thick Australian accent. She always knew how to make me laugh when I needed it the most.

Waiting in the second queue of the day, my number was finally called by a man in the last of the five audition rooms. I walked past the other four rooms and I saw other performers waiting in their own lines, belting out tunes, practising and humming either off key, too loud or just downright awfully. Another guy was exiting from the room I was headed towards, the fifth audition room, and was walking towards me. "Mate, you picked the worst room to be in. They're fucking pricks. Room one and two let me in last year. This room's fucked. Apparently it's one of the head assholes in charge... Good luck, ha!" He tipped his cowboy hat and kept walking, muttering to the others as he left.

That's okay. Cool. I picked the strictest room, the worst of the lot. Or maybe this guy was just a sore loser. I had no way of knowing.

With my nerves at their highest, I walked inside the tiny room with a huge glass window on the opposite side of the door. In front of me was a man in his thirties with several dossier of documents piled on the table in front of him, and a video camera. Writing down my sticker number, he mumbled, "Ok, what are you singing today?”

He did not look up at me once!

“I’ll be singing ‘When Angels Cry’ by The Duke.” I responded.

“Cool, when you’re ready.”

This bearded loser wasn’t even going to acknowledge me. To him I was just another sticker on a long list of stickers that were coming and going. I looked around the room and scanned the habitat this crab was sitting in, a fan blew in his direction. His chair looked comfortable and settling. Here he was in as much comfort as the day could offer and in the meantime, the girls and I had been standing for four hours. He was dressed in hipster-like clothes that matched his reddish coloured beard. This crab seemed like an Indie hip kind of guy, so I knew that my odds were probably against me singing something by ‘The Duke’ who was 80s’ pop royalty. His hair was slicked to one side, moving slightly over his eyes as he moved to turn on the video recorder.

He still didn’t look up.

Running inside my head were a thousand words. I was analysing everything, as usual, when I should have been focusing on what I was about to do. I couldn’t fuck this up. I needed to deliver.

Staring at the base of his head, because his eyes never left the table, I began. My singing was a little above average and as I performed a few trills and runs, his head began to lift. Holding a fairly high note, his attention was grasped and I knew I was ready to go in for the kill.

Rapping isn’t something I have always done, but as I realised more and more songs on the radio were incorporating rap and urban vibes, I knew I had to add this to my bag of skills. I mastered the genre just as well as my pop tracks and my ballads… possibly even better.

> *Aerial King as sharp as knife wing,*
> *I can see the shot on the back of my ring,*
> *Witches in masks they baking with icing,*
> *Preying like a vulture tonight-ah with sin*

It was a rap about me being a bird, an aerial king. I spat out the lyrics like a demon, sharp and on point. As I reached the halfway point of my rap, The Crab speedily began writing notes about my performance and reached his hand to the pile of yellow tickets on the corner of the table.

After I'd finished, he asked me a few more questions about who I was and what I did and then sent me upstairs to the producers. I was excited, but tried not to get overwrought with any feelings. This was, as Belle had informed me, only round one, there was still a long way to go.

I walked back downstairs to grab my bag and saw Drita in the crowd listening to her MP3 player, blocking out the noise around her.

"Dreets, I made it! I have to go upstairs," I rushed, "See you soon!"

Her face was hilarious. The poor thing had endured hours of waiting for me, tolerating thousands of competitors 'practising' and yelling, while mothers screamed at their children to get ready or to fix their make-up. Besides Drita, a robust girl was on the phone to what sounded like her mother. She was half sobbing, half laughing, her blaring voice resonated around all of us.

"Mummy! I've made it through the first round! Can you believe it? I can't wait to share the news with Nan and Pop."

Eavesdropping... I was eavesdropping, as usual. I listened to the rest of her conversation as she proceeded to tell the person on the receiving end, that she was going to meet them at a nearby hospital after she was done. My day's endeavours seemed irrelevant to what this girl was going through. I dislike comparing the intensity of somebody's misfortunes or measuring the relevance of their problems, but seeing this girl made me empathetic. I knew exactly what she was feeling. I had felt it before: happiness with an ever so present spin of sadness as well. It's quite a paradoxical feeling that you can't really express with words.

I passed a group of Star Power employees as I walked upstairs and they were feverishly arguing with one of the contestants. I spotted Belle sitting in a seat near an arched hallway entrance just above the staircase. At the top of the stairs was another table with more Star Power staff. A security guard asked to see my ticket and ushered me in their direction. It was there that I was bombarded with more paperwork: release forms, aptitude tests, confidentiality agreements and more. One of the papers even assessed me to see if I had psychological problems. I recall one of the questions: 'Have you ever had the urge to hurt someone intentionally?' Wow! What the heck was I filling out?

After they took my photograph for their files, I handed them my learner's permit and completed the documents I was given. I sat next to Belle, who was also waiting her turn inside. Before I could speak to her again, a thin bald man wearing crescent shaped glasses opened the door and called her name. I whispered a quick good luck and moved into the next ordered seat. While I was seated, I noticed an unpleasant incident in the direction of the Star Power employees who were seated on the stairway. Perched close to its balcony, the team overlooked the path the yellow ticket-winners were forced to walk on to get upstairs. I had noticed these staff members on my way up the stairs, but had given them no consideration. Closely watching, however, I saw how they were allowing some people to carry on walking upstairs without a problem, ticking a white sheet of paper if they were satisfied, but with others, they would holler at the contestant to totter over and so they could take the contestant's ticket away. I wasn't sure what this was until the same robust girl who I had overheard on the phone earlier began crying. Her glasses were fogged up from tears and her red, tousled hair was dampened with sweat. In a futile attempt to relieve her frustration, she tried to knock one of the tables over and then ran towards the exit, holding her head in her hands. Next in their line of their fire was a gorgeous girl with blonde curls and a fake tan the colour of carrots. They smiled, as they had to me, and allowed her to continue walking past without a problem. It was then that I realised that we had all been filtered again on our way up the stairs. This time we were filtered in or out simply on how we looked: our hair, our skin, our sense of fashion and how we carried ourselves.

Before I was able to fully comprehend what had happened, the bald man popped out of the room and called my name: "NOA!"

Chapter Two

Angels Do Not Cry, They Sing

I felt like a hunted animal. Predators surrounded me. Their eyes fixated on me like vultures about to swoop down and feast on their prey. I looked up and tried to run, but it was too late. They cawed around me and I was stuck. They choked on spit of laughter and plotted my death. It only takes one decision. Sometimes, a decision changes your life entirely... One decision changed mine.

*

Collecting my thoughts, I hopped up from my chair and grabbed the handle of the door that the man had left to close on its own. One foot was barely inside the room. I rested momentarily on my back foot, looking around outside the room one last time before entering. I calmed myself, took a giant breath and entered, gripping onto the metal door handle too tightly.

As soon as I stepped inside that room, a ghastly chill enveloped me. Initially I thought it was nerves, but after a moment I realised that it was just the air conditioning.

Air conditioning! I almost laughed. While thousands of contestants sat outside in the boiling summer heat, a panel of producers sat comfortably in leather computer chairs with ivory cushions and a stunning light hanging from the ceiling. Comfortably cool!

No one spoke to me. I wiped the sweat from my brow and proceeded to a black, X-shaped mark on the floor where I assumed I was supposed to stand. My nerves had gotten the better of me and I continued to sweat. A mantra ran through my head: *Please don't let my make-up run... Please don't let my make-up run...*

I patted my face, took off my jacket to cool down and flung it to the floor. I opened my mouth and heard verbal vomit escaping, like a plague out of Exodus, "Oh, you guys seem comfortable in here with the nice air conditioning and nice little chairs. How are you doing today?"

Sometimes my candour gets me into trouble. I was just trying to appear chilled and conversational, but in reality, especially if you didn't know me, my comments could have sounded full of attitude and sarcasm. They responded with a combination of groans, mumbles and fake laughter. "Haha, yeah we're pretty lucky..."

Crap! Well, that didn't help my nerves!

They glanced at one another, already beginning to judge me without any further exchange of words. We all know that split second assessment of someone based on nothing more than the way they look, how they stand, a few nervously uttered words. I stood there uncomfortably as they rolled their eyes and made their assumptions.

Awkward!

Five of them sat in front of me. There were five producers in all. Five people I had to impress.

I didn't know it at the time, but the five producers essentially represented five different industry divisions: Music and Sound Engineering, Fashion and Styling, Personality and Character Evaluation, Editing and Storylines, and Money, Money and more Money.

To the far left of the panel was the style and fashion producer who was the first to begin the conversation after my dreadful attempt at making a good impression.

"Wow! You look amazing, who are you wearing? I love it!"

"Thanks... I'm wearing Jeremy Scott, from head to toe!"

I was proud to say that. Not many people knew his design aesthetic or knew of him in Australia. This conversation starter helped me find my centre, helped ground me, reminding me of my unique qualities and reigniting my sense of confidence.

"I absolutely love the little teddy bears on your shoes! You could be a stylist for the show."

Her comment was flattering, but also got me thinking... Perhaps if they hated my singing, I *could* get a job as a stylist. I've always loved fashion and everybody knows that style goes hand in hand with music. It was not an impossible assumption for her to make, but that's not why I was here.

I snapped out of the daze I had incidentally mustered and replied with a cordial thank you, looking around the room, waiting, as they shuffled their papers and found my documents. These, from what I could see, were the forms I completed, along with my head shot that the Star Power crew had taken earlier outside.

Focus, NOA! Focus.

"So, you've been on Kitty Kat Sundays? It says here that you have had a lot of experience in the music industry," said the producer on the far right. "Can you elaborate?"

This particular producer was in charge of editing and I now know that he probably wanted footage from my old show. His job was to extrapolate a good enough storyline from me that would be suitable and interesting enough to air on the show.

I explained to him how I had been signed to an underground label from a young age and had been on Kitty Kat Sundays when I was a kid. He listened closely to what I told him and asked me if I had a USB of any old footage of me singing or being on the show.

Of course I did! I had prepared a few files in case I was faced with a situation like this. I pulled out a white USB with my name on it and handed it over to him. This contained: a few songs, some pictures, a video of me on the show and some old homemade music videos from when I was younger.

"Thanks!" he said, too excitedly. "I can't wait to have a look!"

So far I felt as though I had satisfied two out of the five producers: the fashion producer loved my style and the editor had a storyline to cut for television.

The women second on the left had been writing down notes on a piece of paper as we were chatting. After I had spoken to the first two producers, she asked me to tell her a little bit about myself.

"I'm nineteen. I am a student living in Western Sydney. I tutor English to students in high school and I teach dance on the side. I know I'm good at what I do, I just haven't had the opportunity yet to show people. I've been in the industry for a while, behind the scenes. I've written songs for other people and was signed myself at a young age. I know I have that Star Power quality and I want to win."

She seemed impressed: her eyebrows raised, she smiled and nodded her head. She asked me a few more questions about who my influences were and who I aspired to emulate. My quest for success has never simply been about having one song released and making money from it. It's so much more than that. I dream to be like Michael Jackson, the first male, pop megastar; or Madonna, the first female to reinvent herself so many times through the years ensuring she remained relevant. I've always wanted to make a difference in the world: to prove something to all the kids out there who were stuck, that anything can be achieved if you believe in yourself.

Following my third interrogative chat, the second last producer, the man in charge of music and engineering, asked me to repeat the song I had sung to the man downstairs. Okay, this is it!

Once again, I belted out the song resplendently and when the rap came up, I saw their eyes flicker. I could see their clinical minds working overtime, almost mechanically. You see, when industry people meet talent, they see money. They don't simply hear the singer or notice the song itself: they assess, they analyse, they run the odds, they calculate. When greedy bastards see money, they see someone they can screw over.

After singing 'When Angels Cry' by The Duke for a second time, the man in the middle of the panel began scratching his head in deep consideration and thought. He hadn't spoken this whole time and I could tell he was the head producer: essentially the one in charge of finances, responsible for the bottom line decision. Basically, his job was making money.

"No. I want to hear something else," he demanded. "I want another option."

Of course I was prepared, I always had a list of songs at the ready, but as my mind scanned for another song, I felt a lump in my throat that I knew was going to be a problem. He had thrown me. His words took me aback. 'No' could mean so many things, could be interpreted in a variety of ways. What did he mean by 'no'? How could I separate what he meant from how I understood the word? Goodness knows I had heard 'no' enough times to form my own understanding of what it meant to me. But what exactly did 'no' mean anyway?

*

I was fifteen.

Every Monday my singing teacher, Coral, from Purple Voices Singing Schools, would begin by forcing me to sing scales followed by a rendition of whatever song I had planned to sing for that week.

She would say, "Your voice needs repetitive scales to strengthen it; it's basically practising a strange type of 'muscle memory'. You practise your scales and notes over and over and over until you strengthen your pitch, making sure each note sounds perfect and precise."

It might strengthen your muscle memory, but singing all these notes each week doesn't help you to improve your vocal range. Imagine doing 500 sit-ups every day. Sure your abdomen becomes stronger, but your abdomen is the only thing that's getting a work out. I realise now that, at that time, I should have been pushing myself to sing notes that were unreachable for me and to sing harder songs. I should have been trying to sing a little higher and a little lower every week. That's when muscle memory kicks in... when you hit that high note and realise *SHIT! I can do it!* When you actually acknowledge that you've already reached that note before and so, of course, it's possible to do it again. Once you've strengthened that note, you move on up to the next note, and then the next... and so on. Yet at that age, it was difficult to force a song outside my comfort zone without my voice breaking. *Bloody adolescence!* But now, standing in front of this powerful producer, I wished Coral had focused on my range a little more each week, and a little less on just singing scales.

I had only been at the singing school and working with Coral for a few weeks when a 'Master Class' opportunity came up. It's funny how, as a child, adults can manipulate the way you think and your thought processes. I have experienced this myself as an English tutor, always twisting words to make students believe something is a 'bigger deal' than it really is, or convincing them it's 'the best thing' to do for their education. The same situation happens in this music world. I was told by Coral that it would be a great opportunity to go to this Master Class as the Principal of the Purple Voices Singing Schools would be in attendance. Little did I know that it was just a ploy to make a few hundred bucks. But I'm not the type of person to be happy to pay my hundred and simply walk away. No way!

Every child who goes to an entertainment education institution is told that they're going to be a star... But at the end of the day, the fact of the matter is that only one out of the whole institution will ever make it past the finished line. Not to forget that when it comes to the music industry there's new talent pouring in every day. You cross the finish line only to begin another race. This is just like a gymnast, I guess. Those phony sports centers that promise everyone that they're going to get into the Olympics. Let's be real here: that probably isn't going to happen. Truly! It may sound harsh, but there are only a few places on a national team. You can't change the rules and add a fifth member to an Olympic squad of four. This is what is so rarely understood by those on the outside. The number of positions of fame and the possibilities of leaving true legacies in the music industry are numbered. Not everyone can have a place on the pop throne. These places are limited. But the way I was brought up, that has contributed to my (possibly) twisted psychology, is to believe that you should do everything you can to get the most out of your money. I would not let this Master Class become a ploy to rid me of a hundred dollars; I would turn this into another opportunity to get ahead, regardless of the ruse. While everyone else would be focusing on singing and learning, I would be making contacts and providing the school principal with a lasting first impression. To everyone else it would be just a class; albeit a Master Class. For me, it would be playtime and I would use it to my advantage.

The principal of Purple Voices Singing Schools was looking to make money, just like the producer who sat in front of me now. These producers didn't care about me as a person. I'd seen that same look before. The position I was in now was exactly like the one I had been in at that Master Class.

Looking back, I realise how much I blended in with everyone else, compared to how I look now. Brown hair, old clothes, nothing special. Just the typical ethnic boy with a voice: *boring*. But that's the point I'm trying to make here. Okay, so I could sing, but I wasn't anything special on the aesthetic scale back then. I didn't have an 'image' or 'branding', but I managed to get people interested nonetheless. I tell people all the time that in situations like this, it's in the blood. From a young age, I could walk into a room and people would stare at me. I never knew why and to be honest I still don't. Today, however, it's a different story. People notice me, and it's obvious why they look: bleached blonde hair and sassy attitude, but back then... why did they stare? Why did their eyes lock onto me? Why did they sit there gazing? Sometimes I think it's because I was born to be a star and people instinctively knew there was something sparkly and shiny about me, compared to everyone else. Okay, so I know this sounds 99% delusional, but I truly believe God graces all of us with a little sugar and spice... maybe I have a little more spice than everyone else.

It was on the day of the Master Class that I encountered important faces that would change my singing career forever. This past experience sat in exact parallel to the situation I found myself in now, standing here in front of this powerful producer. My main important reason for going to the Master Class was Darryl Spade: the principal of Purple Voices Singing Schools, and the one person who could offer a recording contract. Where was I now? In exactly the same position: in front of the one person who could determine the course of my future.

Sitting at the piano, as we all walked into the classroom that day, was Darryl Spade. Gospel trills spat out of his mouth like a fiery dragon, illuminating the room and silencing the class. He was a magnificent performer. With every note and every whimsical manipulation of the voice, he was able to grasp our full attention vocally. I understand now that the reason he became a teacher was because he had never made it himself: those who fail, teach. That's a key thing to remember. Those who teach, often know their craft because they've failed to reach their imagined potential. Sure, Darryl had released a few gospel EPs and albums, but who wants to hear Australian-based Darryl Spade when we can listen to Ray Charles or Stevie Wonder? You have to have the right amount of uniqueness, nerve and talent to succeed in this business. Darryl had talent, but was lacking nerve and uniqueness. And the producer right in front of me now? He definitely had nerve... but no talent. (Unless you call intimidating kids a talent.)

Still scanning for the right song to sing, my mind kept flooding back to the Darryl situation. I remembered how everyone in the Master Class began by singing a few vocal exercises together. I've committed to memory that the notes and exercises got higher and that I couldn't keep up...

La la la la Lo lo Le Li La
Lo lo lo lo li la lo li Le
Le le le.....

Nope. That wasn't going to happen. I remember looking around the room to see that more than half of the students had dropped out of the race before me. There were a handful of female 'typical pop' singers still reaching the higher notes. Slowly, but without a fight, they dropped out too, leaving a young ethnic looking girl with dark brown hair, a hooked nose and bright illuminating eyes standing in front of Darryl, belting out the higher exercises alone. She definitely had nerve and talent. However, I know now that unfortunately she did not have any uniqueness in her image... But then again, neither did I at the time. This girl continued singing alone for about three exercises as we all watched in amazement.

"Bravo, Arianne!" Darryl praised her. "Let's hear it for this beautiful gem, everyone clap your hands together!" We all began clapping, except my clap was more of a withheld, limp seal clap — I was jealous.

"Arianne... Sing that run we practised last month for the kids," Darryl ordered.

She began belting out some fancy, minor run that had an ethnic sounding twist to it. Her voice was a twist of Shakira meets Christina Aguilera and unfortunately, in our world, if you already sound like someone else you are no longer unique. This sucks because Arianne, as it turns out, is a hardworking and talented musician and vocalist. However, nobody I know works as hard as I do to 'make it'. But then again, maybe I'm just egotistical and judgmental.

Arianne was Darryl's favourite pupil in Sydney and it was obvious to everyone in the room that they had a great relationship, not only a business relationship, but a personal one. The smiles, high-fives and hugs that were coming out of the pair of them that day were unaccountable. We knew she was the best singer because more time was spent on her than anybody else. The teachers at the school were interested in her because she was the most talented. Therefore, they would help and nurture her talent because this would hopefully mean that they would be successful for having assisted her. At the end of the day, humans are drawn to those they feel they will gain something from. I have no doubt that the faculty at the school loved and cared for Arianne, however, the reason they loved and cared for her that much was because there was a slim chance that she may have become successful, and out of all the students in the school, she was deemed to have the highest chance. In any case, that's what the people at Star Power wanted too. They wanted to raise the status of somebody they could manipulate in order to have their ulterior motives come to fruition. It was the same old story.

Witnessing social exchanges between Arianne and Darryl, I knew that I had to be in his good books as well. Move over, Arianne... Hello George (remembering that the persona NOA did not exist yet). I actually found it quite mindboggling that other vocalists in the Master Class did not care that Arianne was getting special treatment. Perhaps they were oblivious to it, after all, Darryl had a sort of eloquence about him. He was very articulate when speaking and had a very regal demeanor. Maybe it was his deeply religious singing or his convicting gospel cries, I'm not sure.

After a few vocal drills, we were asked to stand up, one at a time, and sing the small piece we had prepared. Sitting through about half an hour of off-pitched wails and whale-sounding screeches, I realised that, at the end of the day, business is money. If Darryl and Coral wanted to run a successful business they would need funds. Funds meant that they had to falsely provide dreams to poor-voiced children and their parents in order to keep the school going. This twisted situation meant providing services to talentless children and fitting them with a dream to boot! Out of all the kids in this Master Class, the only people I saw who were going to 'get anywhere' were Arianne or myself. Notice the use of the word 'or'.

Compare that to Star Power. If they wanted to keep their seasons going, they too needed funds and ratings. So obviously this nameless head producer wanted to hear more from me.

I was called forth and was given the microphone by Darryl. From what I can recall, he looked at me and passed judgment before he even heard me sing at all. To him, I assume, I was probably one of the 'average' kids who were going to sing slightly flat and off pitch followed by a staged round of applause by the teachers to keep me coming back and spending money. That was not the case. I placed the microphone to my mouth and began to sing.

I threw what Coral had taught me out the window. I wasn't going to sing a hit pop song by Rihanna. This guy loved Jesus, so I was going to give him Jesus.

It's been months, since you went away; left with no words, nothing to say. I lent you my heart and soul. But it wasn't good enough for you, so I ask God to send me an angel...

Silence. Obviously stunned.

"Wow! I did not expect that... How old are you?" Darryl asked.

"I'm fifteen." I told him.

"Interesting. I can't wait to see your next performance."

Hooked.

Just like I had been then, I was stuck in front of this producer now and needed another trick.

I looked beneath the table of the producer panel in front of me and noticed this producer's bag lying beneath his feet. On his bag were several rock band badges and stickers that one might see on a young rebellious teenager's bag who wanted the world to be filled with anarchy.

Light bulb!

Clearly this guy was into rock.

Clearing my throat I said, "I'm not used to singing this genre, but I know myself to be very versatile when it comes to music... So, I'll be singing a rock song by The Rolling Stones."

Hooked again.

Chapter Three

The Bullet of Technology

Technology is fast-paced and ever-changing, but today this change seems to occur more rapidly than ever before. Once upon a time, books were the realm of paper, but now, well, some of you are probably reading this on a tablet or your phone. We have come to rely on technology to the point of dependency—try going off-grid for a few days and see how dependent you have become! As a performer, technology is ever-present: in the studio, on stage and even in private quotidian settings. The wait for the latest upgrade in any software these days has the world on tenterhooks. But what if you could get a software update for your whole life? What if someone came to you with a file that could just upgrade you? What if you could become 'You Mark 2' in an instant? What would you do?

*

After I returned home on the evening of the Star Power auditions, I ran into the living room to tell my mother about where I had really been. Like any ethnic child, I copped a lecture, a warning and a verbal beat down for not telling her the truth in the first place, but then, after all the bother of emotions, I recall Mum giving me this particular look. I remember that look like it was yesterday. It was a look she had given me before. This is the look that only a parent can give their child: when the architect stares at the progeny. Even now, I just can't describe in words the love that I saw in in her eyes at that moment. All I can say is that this is the look of a parent who wishes the very best for their child and who, in that moment, hopes and prays to God that their child will be okay and will fulfil their dreams.

"So what happens now?" she asked, wiping her hands with a paper towel.

"I wait for an email or a phone call...?" I told her, contemplating, "I'm not too sure, I don't know how it works exactly..."

The wait for this call was heinous at best. Apprehension, in situations like this, takes you over completely. Every waking moment has you thinking about the one thing you're waiting for. Literally. Every. Single. Moment. I was a wreck!

Sleep: Star Power. Train rides: Star Power. Dance class: Star Power. Vocal Coaching: Star Power. Work: Star Power. Out with friends: Star Power. Out with family: Star Power. In the car: Star Power. Star Power... Star Power... Star Power.

Sometimes I opened my mouth and words came out like verbal diarrhoea. It was all I could think about and all I could talk about. I talked about it with anyone who would listen, and to be honest, I still talk about it to this day. I could be in a conversation about birds and somehow the conversation can wind back to how a bird 'symbolically' flew past me on the day of the audition. Conspiracy theories enveloped all of my conversations and anxiety didn't help but heighten these theories.

But what if they absolutely hated it? But I did a pretty good job, surely they liked it? I don't know when they'll let me know, do you think it's been too long? A group of girls I met there already got a phone call... when will mine come...? I'm probably on the bottom end of the list because my name starts with N? Are they going to call me or email me? What if my phone dies or my email doesn't work?

I was dogged by these thoughts. On and on they went. It was dreadful.

Despite a saturation of technology, there can still be a gaping fear of being uncontactable. Sometimes, that's just the case.

*

Every year, Darryl Spade from Purple Voices Singing Schools held annual concerts where the elite performers from each of his suburban schools would come together to perform a concert. From the very first year I started at his singing school, I had been asked to perform. In my first year, I had written my first song with my now ex-manager and producer Ted. The song was pretty urban and had a lot of funk to it. At that time, I felt there was a huge amount of tension between Darryl and Ted. It would be a few years later that I would finally get to the bottom of that animosity. So, my performance for Darryl that first year was somewhat of an unconcern to him. If Ted had worked on it, Darryl simply didn't care for it.

The following year, I had just turned sixteen before being asked to perform at the annual concert again. Things were different that time though, I had watched Ted and Darryl's business relationship become closer as Ted moved into the role of deputy at the school, and I knew that there was something going on in the business between the two of them. I'm not sure if it was the tightly gripped handshakes between them or the Cheshire cat smiles, but my intuition told me something was going on and that their 'friendship' wasn't as real as they portrayed.

At this time, I was obsessed with a singer who was booming all of the world, soaring up the charts globally: Lady Gaga. She was something fresh and innovative, she challenged the status quo and prompted rebellion and social change. I admired her dearly. I bought all her records, learnt all her dance moves, purchased all the merchandise available to me and had a collection of magazines with her face on the cover.

That year, the song that I wrote for the end of year concert was a song that continues to shape me into the person that I am today. Over time, this song has seen several producers work on it and has been subject to rewriting a minimum of fifty times before its official release. Despite the intensive revision, the song's central message still remains the same.

Villain: a character whose evil actions or motives are important to a plot.

This one word 'villain' captures the essence of who I have been for most of my life. To many people in the industry, my motives and actions have appeared selfish, arrogant, rude and somewhat evil. To others, my actions have been brave, courageous and valiant. This is what I most admire in a villain... it's all about perception. But now I'm getting off track... more on this later.

The song was something incredibly unique and very different. It blended 80s' funk, pop and urban Hip-Hop all in one melodic fusion. The performance involved black capes, dancers with wings, chartreuse-coloured snakeskin airbrushed make-up and wild tresses complimenting daunting yellow contact lenses.

That night was actually a very significant awakening for me. Awards were given, as usual, to those who showed improvement or exceptional artistic talent, and I waited to receive this award like I had the year prior. After the award ceremony, there would be a six-week vacation before the next year's unrelenting enrolment. But this year was different...

Daryl stepped up to the microphone to thank everyone for coming and to congratulate all of the performers. "I don't usually do this, but tonight I have been extraordinarily impressed with such remarkable talent in the room. I cannot let this student go unnoticed. This performer's originality, dedication and passion has spoken deeply to me... God calls for occasions like these ones and it is with my pleasure that I call George up onto the stage tonight..."

I remember I hadn't even been paying attention. I was in the middle of taking off my boots that had rubbed on my skin during my performance; I had a huge blister beneath one the toes on my left foot. I was complaining to my Aunt Kathy about wearing uncomfortable clothing while performing, but having to do it anyway so you look your best.

When Daryl called my name out, I felt all eyes on me. Everyone in the room was looking my way and curiously waiting to find out why I was being called to the stage and why I had even been pointed out. I stood up, pressed my foot back into my boot and ignored the pain. I walked up the stairs and stood on the mounted platform on the stage next to Darryl.

"I've seen George grow so rapidly in such a short amount of time at this school. I have to say, he has been a tremendous asset to my vocal coaching franchise and I see big things in the near future from this handsome young man...." He paused as everyone began clapping.

There's a very strange phenomenon that occurs when people give me compliments. Many people are not good at accepting compliments, many people find it excruciating to hear praise. I call this, in my terms: the most awkward and embarrassing thing in my life!

Perhaps it's because I wasn't brought up with affection, but compliments always make me feel uneasy and uncomfortable. To lead into an example, I remember, a few years ago, dating this particular girl. She told me I had silky hair and a cute smile and that all the girls in the nightclub would be all over me if she weren't there next to me. I immediately felt squeamish and deflected her compliment awkwardly back at her. "Yeah, I guess you have nice eyes?" Seriously, it was that bad. When faced with a compliment, I'm terrible.

I do accept more impersonal, unemotional responses though and with great success. Any compliment about my music, fashion choices or style and I will 100% agree, I take these compliments well because hard work deserves recognition... and I work doggedly at my craft. It's like getting your homework back corrected, there's a tick or a cross if you get it right or wrong. That's fine, I can take that. But to compliment my character is something else. These compliments are much more personal and make me feel open and vulnerable. Like somehow if you compliment me, then you have the power to hurt me just the same...

Nevertheless, after Daryl was forced to wait while my howling and whistling wog[2] family piped down, he opened his mouth again to warp my world into

---

2 An Australian term for non-Anglo European, e.g. Greek, Italian, Balkan, Slavic.

something completely different.

"I would like to extend an offer to Mr George here tonight. I would like to personally forward your original song to the head of Juicebox Music in London, in hope that they see the same talent in you that I do. Congratulations. I'm very proud to call you my student."

I was being offered a software upgrade, in that very moment up there on that stage. I was an old radiophone from the 1920s being offered a Smartphone upgrade. To this day, I still flashback and think, *what the actual heck?* I still find it almost incomprehensible. But of course, no villain's trajectory is that straightforward, there's always more, there are always twists and turns as the villain plunges headlong toward the end of the story.

After Daryl contacted Juicebox Music, I was put in touch with a Mr Tim Quarter, who was the Chief Executive Officer of the record label. There were two months of negotiations and deliberations that were a hell I would not wish on anyone.

At sixteen, you know what you want, but I guess you are still very impulsive and, because you've never lost anything, you feel like you have nothing to lose. You don't know the price of putting yourself out there and what you're capable of losing.

Tim Quarter, the head of Juicebox Music was a shark, an old shark. He had worked with many of Australia's first pop icons of the nineties: Vanessa Amorosi, Holly Valance and Stephanie Macintosh. Back in those days, there were not many TV competitions and it was much easier to promote anybody to fame via radio and CD single sales.

My agreement with Juicebox Music London began with Tim requesting the lump sum of eleven thousand dollars.

His email to me read:

> *Hi George,*
> *We received an email from Darryl about your progress as a serious musician at his company. We're very excited to work with you. The highlighted area would be shared costs, equally split between Juicebox Music and yourself. Legal information will be sent to you as soon as Tim is back from his trip. If you have any questions don't hesitate to ask.*
> *Annette*
> *Assistant to Tim Quarter*

I remember looking at the attached monetary split and crying. There was no way I was going to be able to pay that much money.

After shedding many tears and uttering several frustrated screams, I came to the conclusion that, financially, this wasn't going to happen. I responded to the email with a sincere apology, mentioning that had I been in possession of eleven thousand, I would have willingly signed up.

That email was all I could think about for the coming weeks. Tim had ideas to put me in a studio with a famous female vocalist in London and to record an album in a two-week span that he had put aside just for me. These were all the things I had once dreamed of doing. There were two things at this time that actually stunned me: a) I was being offered something like this in the first place, and b) that I wasn't taking up this opportunity. We, as a family, simply couldn't afford it.

Not many people can comprehend scenarios like this one. At such a young age, being offered your whole dream in one email, and in the same twenty-four hours having that dream come crushing down like an avalanche. It wasn't fun.

I received a reply from Tim:

> *George,*
> *Oh, dear! What a shame—we were so excited too!*
> *Anyway,*
> *Tim*

'Anyway'... It was like he didn't even care. Oh, dear, for me, but no care for him! I struggled with this outcome for several weeks. I was inconsolable. I sat alone at lunch at school and distanced myself from everybody except my girlfriend. She was probably the only person I could talk to at that time. Even Darryl left me out high and dry on this occasion. I had emailed him asking if there was any way he could sponsor my trip or find another contact here in Sydney. *No response.*

After all, wasn't I his student, his shining star? I guess not. It was Coral who was my vocal coach; Darryl just owned the business. He had never taught me by myself, ever. So I guessed he wasn't really invested, he didn't care. Added to this, Ted had been removed as deputy of the school a few days before. Their business relationship had obviously soured, which meant that my relevance to Darryl was back to zero.

I began questioning myself: Was I even chosen because of my talent, because I was good, or was this all a plotline in a story of conflict between Ted and Darryl?

*

A month passed by and I waited for something to happen. Just when I had given up hope, I received a phone call and an email on the same night. At the time I assumed it was coincidence, but looking back now, it kind of adds up.

The email was from Tim and it read:

> *Hey George,*
> *I have been through your situation again to see if there is any way we can do this and I might have found a co-investor who just may agree to co-fund you in some degree, later in the year...*
> *I will come back to you next week.*
> *Tim*

Immediately, I dropped to my knees and thanked God with every particle of my body. Literally, I was praying on the floor when my phone rang...

"Hello?" I answered.

"Hey. Gee, it's me, Ted. I need to see you and your mother right away. Could you come in tomorrow night for a chat at 8pm?"

To be honest, I remember thinking, *Shit, they're kicking me out for something!*

I answered demurely calm, "Umm, sure... Is everything ok?"

"Yeah, everything is fine bro, very excited, see you soon!"

I went to bed that night wandering if Tim would find the investor and speculating about what Ted wanted. I always hated my mother getting involved in the business side of things with my music, and Ted knew this, so I was curious why he would ask her to be present too.

*

Walking into the music school that night with my mother, I was simultaneously nervous and anxious. All the students had finished up lessons for the night, and Ted and his wife ushered us into the waiting foyer to sit with them on the couches.

After a quick catch-up chat, Ted got down to business.

"We want to offer George... NOA... Whichever one best suits this conversation... Something special, something we've never offered any other student here..."

I recall my mum's face lighting up with excitement. Although young, I knew not to get too excited until hearing what proposal or actual offer was being made.

Ted continued, "This will be separate to Darryl Spade's school and has no affiliation to the classes or the business that is run here... I am starting my own business: 'Teddy Productions', and I'd like George to be the first person I sign. This means free recording and producing at all times, but profits and copyright will be split forty-sixty. Don't give me an answer now. This is something I recommend you sleep on, but I'd like to get started as soon as possible to get some songs out there... This also means that you will not pay for any vocal or song writing lessons that you have previously been paying for at this school."

Who was hooking whom?

My mum, a typical ethnic mother, literally jumped on the poor man and his wife and started to kiss and thank them for the opportunity they were giving her child. She really couldn't afford to send me there and had picked up an extra shift at the takeaway shop to raise the funds. To her, this was like a gift from Jesus.

I was excited, but also had Tim and London playing in the back of my head. Ted was one of my confidants so I had already shared with him what was going on with Tim and Juicebox Music.

"What about London?" I asked nervously. Three heads turned around to stare back at me in shock.

Recalling this now, I distinctly remember their faces in somewhat shocked disfiguration: *I'm sorry. Is a sixteen year old not allowed to speak at a meeting regarding their own future?*

"Well..." retorted Ted, "If you do choose to go to London, then this offer is obviously void. I know it's a big decision, but it's up to you which path you'd like to take. A path with care... I mean, we've known you for a long time... Or a path with risk." He placed his arms around his wife and smiled at me with confidence.

I respected Ted. He had played the family card on me. Family: that sense of security and safety that I had not felt and that I always wanted. Holding his wife's arms, he was looking to 'adopt' me into his musical family. His choice of the word *risk* was also clever, in encouraging me to assume the risk was only being taken on one side. But let's be clear here, risks are taken every day, in every situation we find ourselves in. No decision is risk-free.

Leaving me with a week to decide, Ted Dand his wife kissed my mother and myself goodnight, and left us with a decision to make.

I considered all aspects: If I stayed in Australia, I could be with my family and also stay in school. I could record in the afternoons and juggle everything else that was going on in my life. If I moved to London, I would be uprooting my whole life for this crazy risk. At least if the risks I took were made in Australia, I'd have my education to fall back on and, to be honest, I was scared of the sharks that swam in the deep overseas waters.

To this day I can't help but feel regret, every now and then, as I think about what might have happened if I did take that dive. But I'm glad I didn't. I know I would have drowned.

I wasn't stupid though; I waited for Tim's email before I made my decision. The next week came with no response from him and I needed to answer to Ted as soon as possible.

"Yes, I will sign to your company here in Sydney and I'm glad to begin working with you," I responded to Ted in my next song writing class.

Ted was over the moon and I was enthusiastic, but still scared about what was to come.

What I was unaware of at the time was that the only reason Ted had offered me this position was so that he could snatch me away from Darryl and also from Tim. Although Tim was not connected directly to Darryl, if I had 'made it' with him, it would be due to Darryl's connections and I would be Darryl's find. As the business relationship between Ted and Darryl was diminishing, I guess his ego needed a win. Ted had heard about Tim's offer and in this business and when one shark sees another shark going in for a feed, they swim in for the kill as well. It can be a real feeding frenzy! Sometimes, they may have not thought you were even worth anything, but if someone else sparks the fire of want, if they desire you, then there's always someone else who decides they want you too.

Looking back, I guess I did make a good decision because I never heard from Tim regarding that matter again. No investor was found and no one was in contact with me regarding negotiations. I thank God I chose at least one avenue that was on offer.

And with all this past experience of waiting for a response from these industry sharks, my fear of not hearing back from Star Power was ever-present. I knew the wait all too well. I didn't have a second choice to fall back on, just like I didn't back then. It was either getting the call from Star Power, or continuing to work as a dance teacher while busting my arse at university for another year, struggling to make ends meet. I had been ignored before, who was to say I wouldn't be now.
*

Luckily, after a long wait, I did receive my phone call. It came three weeks after they told me I would hear back from them.

I was teaching a Hip-Hop class to my group of small boys when my phone began buzzing. I paused the music and stared down at the unknown landline number.

Sliding my answer button, I picked up the phone assuming it was a wrong number.

"Hi, this is Jemima from Star Power, how are you doing today NOA?"

Startled, I hushed the boys and stepped outside while ushering one of the younger student teachers in to take over my class.

I calmed myself and replied, "I'm good, how are you?"

"Not too bad, we're actually just calling to see if we can get some more information about yourself for our records…"

"Yeah? Cool, no worries. What were you after?"

The woman on the phone proceeded to ask me about my personal life, hardships and past music experiences. The phone call lasted about two hours and I was getting very tired of rehashing the past. I didn't know why she was asking all these questions, but I was aware that a lot of these music variety shows present the public with a sob story past from contestants in order to evoke sympathy and admiration from their viewers.

I milked my story, telling the woman about my father, who to this day has never seen me perform, and about my childhood that wasn't the loveliest. I told her of being signed to a private label and how I was now standing on my own two feet. She asked about Kitty Kat Sundays and a whole bunch of other questions that I believed weren't really anybody's business… I answered them nonetheless. I mean, what choice did I have?

"Thank you so much NOA! We will get back to you if you have progressed further."

Beep!

What? Was that just another round of eliminations over the phone? After weeks of waiting and apprehension, they had just called me to ask me more questions and to leave me with no answers.

I didn't know how to feel about this… I was happy that they called, that they had contacted me, but they didn't exactly give me anything of value. Once again I was left to wait on another uncertainty.

The words resonated in my head: *IF you have progressed further…*

I couldn't believe I had to wait again.

If it was to receive a no, I wouldn't even be contacted, I would be forgotten just like that… Just like I had been once before by Tim. I just didn't know how companies could do this to people.

*

It's funny how technology works. Sometimes, technology can remove emotion from a situation. If you're face-to-face with somebody and you ask them a question, it is unlikely that they will simply fail to reply, letting you sit there staring at them in silence…

With an email, this is one hundred percent possible. No emotion. No feeling. No response. No care.

When you're having a face-to-face verbal conversation, you get to witness body language, emotive reactions: a quiver in the lips if that person is lying or nervous, a glance diagonally towards the ground if they're upset or have regrets, a glint of sparkle in their eyes if they're truly excited.

Technology may be constantly upgrading, but there are people who strive to exploit this unemotional source of communication as a way to avoid feeling bad about their decisions. It's easier to ruin someone's life when you're not staring them in the face. An employer can fire someone by signing a piece of paper and then walk off to have a cup of coffee… A lawyer can take somebody's child away by signing over custody via a legal email… Someone can push a button in one room and kill somebody else in another location without the scarring image of them dying. It's that easy. Will guilt haunt their conscience? Perhaps. But it's much harder to pull the trigger when you have someone staring into your soul.

I was used to being held at gunpoint. Were they going to pull the trigger?

Chapter Four

Snakes and Shadows

Shadows are spaces that lie just out of sight. Their darkened depths offer camouflage: places to hide, an abyss where nobody can find you.

Sometimes, having a shadow is a must, a necessity. When you don't want to be in the spotlight, when you need to get away, the depths of a shadow become appealing. When I crave solitude, I am a fan of shadows. Yet sometimes, creeping into them unbeknownst can be a really bad idea. Sometimes you can lose yourself in their dark spaces, and hiding in the shadows for too long can leave you with a definite lack of Vitamin D and a lacklustre life of lost opportunities and missed chances.

*

As it turned out, I had been in the shadows for a prolonged time. I hadn't realised how long I had been hiding out, obscured, concealed, unnoticed, until I suddenly found myself out into the sun again, momentarily dazzled, looking around with amazement and marvelling at the light on my skin. Signing with Ted was my way out of the shadows... or so I thought.

Ted and I decided to sit down and discuss the best route to get my music out to the public. I knew that by putting out as much music as I could, more people would hear my music and consequentially, more people would recognise my voice. My sound is a fascinating mix of the unique and the versatile, it is varied and has the potential for great popularity. I knew it would spread like wildfire; all I needed to do was get it out there.

But this was not what Ted wanted.

Don't get me wrong, we made a lot of music. It just wasn't going anywhere. He never let me release anything.

I sat in the shadows waiting.

Waiting... waiting... waiting...

While I was signed to Ted's label, we wrote around fifty tracks in less than a year: tracks ranging from Electronic Pop, R&B and K-Pop (Korean Pop), even to Hip-Hop and Rap. Ted was very meticulous when it came to business, but he had his own particular ideas about how to move forward and he was very stubborn. I argued with him a lot, but in the end he always managed to convince me to do whatever it was that he wanted. I guess I didn't feel like I had the power to stand my own ground; I felt I had too much to lose if I tried to force my own opinions. I loved the fact that I was spending so much time with Ted and the fact I was in his studio. I bit my tongue and held my words many times. I sacrificed my voice in order to continue to sit at Ted's dinner table and become part of his family. He would drive half an hour, two times a week to pick me up from my home and take me to his studios, where he lived around the corner. I stayed over for dinner often, conversing with his wife and going out for fun activities with the whole studio team. We always had a great time and, because I was lacking this sense of belonging at home, Ted, his wife and my coach Coral, became another family to me. I loved being in Ted's inner circle, and all that came with that... I didn't want to risk losing it by opening my mouth and arguing about what I wanted!

During this time, Ted convinced me that by not releasing a lot of songs, I would be more respected in the music industry. He made me realise that it would be more effective and more successful to release one professional song that was well produced and well written. I did agree with him in this matter, but I felt that there was no point in releasing a professional song when you had no one to hear it yet. I thought it was important to build a fan base first and I thought the way to do this was by singing covers and putting them on YouTube, spreading free downloads for friends and family, and even handing out flyers.

Ted wasn't having any of this.

What felt so frustrating about this time was that I had already started to gain some momentum online with my K-Pop covers and my different renditions of old R&B songs and 80s' tracks that I would remix and put my own twist on, and these successes saw me yearning for more of the same. I kept doing this and, every time I would go behind Ted's back to release something online, he would sit me down and warn me that if I did it again there would be consequences. Two words have stuck with me from these lectures from Ted: *Quality Control.*

To this day (as much as I didn't understand it then) I thank him so much for these two words. Quality control means regulating the standard of your product or service. It means controlling the quality of whatever it is you release to the public, be that images, promotions or tracks. I realised that the quality had to be perfect before anything was released. Quality control... Now this is a great mantra for somebody with a huge following and with a lot of money or a label behind them. But I didn't have any of that.

When you don't have a legitimate big-name-label funding you, *quality control* needs to go out the window and you need to focus on and work every avenue possible to you in order to promote yourself and your music.

At the beginning of this record label relationship between Ted and me, we began by writing songs twice a week at his studios at the singing school. What I now know was that Ted was just beginning with song writing sessions to buy time while he looked for other sponsors and other investors to co-fund his label. He did not have any money whatsoever to help his business, let alone to help me.

He could not help me and so I was going to be in the shadows, whether I liked it or not.

Amidst this time of 'financial hardship in the business', Ted allowed me to do anything I wanted, as long as this didn't conflict with his quality control rules. He let me audition for local competitions and even audition for another large record label in Korea. This Korean audition was different from any of the other auditions I had ever experienced. It was an online audition where contestants had to send through an original song and a cover of a Korean song they had already posted online. The label, satisfied with what I had sent, offered me to fly over to Korea, free of charge, to study music and the Korean entertainment business at their headquarters in the hope of choosing me to debut.

You see, the music industry in Korea is very different to the conventional Western music industry that we all know. Most of the people chosen from these auditions were kids who were selected to move into the headquarters of the record labels in Korea, and who ended up becoming 'trainees' studying to be singers, dancers and actors. They studied every day, every night and every waking hour of their lives... They committed 100% of their time and energy into these companies, for years, in hope they would one day satisfy the companies' CEOs in order to be debuted and have their song released. But nothing was ever guaranteed.

You could be a 'trainee' your whole life there and be stuck in the shadows with nothing but a hopeful spotlight in your dreams.

I was thoroughly aware of the situation and the industry differences in Korea as I had studied K-Pop music in my spare time, specifically a girl group that I was inspired by called 2NE1.

As this point in my life, I found myself at a crossroad of darkness, every path seemingly as shadowy as the next.

I remember my thoughts spiralling out of control like they normally did in situations like these. I tried to play the fortune teller at one point, to 'see' which was the best option for me, I tried to track every possibility to eliminate the greatest risks and maximise the highest number of benefits. If I stayed with Ted, would anything really take off? It had already been a year of writing songs that I wasn't allowed to release... Would anybody ever hear them? Would I get a chance like Ted was offering me again?

On the other hand, I could uproot my whole life and move to Korea where all expenses would be paid for and I would live a luxurious life... But, I would have no guaranteed debut. At least here with Ted, I knew a debut was supposed to come. He wouldn't have signed me without wanting to promote me at some point. Would he? Do you only get one chance at success? What if I made the wrong decision and missed my one and only opportunity? In hindsight, my fortune telling was never going to be right. Does anybody ever know what the future can hold?

With high school finals around the corner, I made the decision, once again, to stay with Ted. I crossed my fingers that this was the best for my future.

*

Arianne and I were very close during this period. I was slowly surpassing her as Coral and Darryl's most successful student at the school and was always bumping into her on my way to record in the hallways. She knew about my business relationship with Ted, but she only knew this because she had begun to teach vocals at the school and I was there recording all the time.

It was inevitable that she would find out, so Ted and Coral had decided to tell her the circumstances. Arianne was such a good singer, so it was inevitable that I would perceive her as a threat who could 'knock me off the block' whenever she wanted to. She had known Coral for over ten years and was even present at Ted and Coral's daughter's wedding. I kept her close because she was a threat to my throne, but also because I loved her company. That was the reality of my thinking at that time, that a friend could also be a threat.

Arianne and I complimented each other as friends immensely. We were each other's sounding board, bouncing ideas back and forth. It was funny because I looked up to her so much. Ever since I had seen her at the Master Class I had wanted to sing like her. I wanted to show people that I could surpass a female vocalist even though I was a male. As we got closer, the feeling of being threatened just became friendly competition, and all the other stupid tension was resolved. Phone calls between the two of us became more frequent and our friendship became strong.

Arianne was very different to me. She grew up in a wealthy family with lots of money. Her father was a businessman and had investments in many companies and fields, from property investments to shares. From my recollection, he even dabbled in small businesses and the food industry and always brought home food from a café the family owned but did not manage. Her father was always on the phone and was always very proper, polite and pleasantly formal.

Her mother complimented her father and was just as perfect. She was always dressed in designer clothing, hair pushed back into a tight bun with perfect make-up: a lovely lady. Arianne's parents were very wealthy, but also very nice. Wealth, manners and warmth: a combination rarely known to those of us in living in suburbia.

*

Ted had also recently found an investor and, without my knowledge, had concocted his own plans: plans that were not the same as mine.

I remember it like it was yesterday. Ted burst through the doors of the singing school screaming at the top of his lungs. "I've done it! I've done it!"

He ushered me into the studio room and proceeded to tell me that our dreams were about to come true: mine and his.

"An investor has funded my label and the project to get you famous! We're going to be rich!"

Finally, I thought, *No more shadows.*

*

Sometimes I laugh at how small the world really is. It's very easy to let yourself hide in the shadows when everyone is connected and when each one of these connections seems to know what you have been up to and has an option about your life. Sometimes you just need to get away.

With money under his belt, Ted decided it would be a great idea to release my first song. As promised, the quality of the song was going to be absolutely amazing and a video clip was in motion.

It was during this time where Ted decided to use his manipulation skills to their fullest potential. Dancers came and danced, back-up singers came and sang, and a lot of meetings were held with different video directors and producers. Somehow, Ted always got the best deal.

I rehearsed for weeks after auditioning my dancers. I recall sweating so much during rehearsals and even crying one night as my feet bled afterwards. I had choreographed everything with my dance teacher, Dustin. I, however, had to teach the dancers alone.

During one rehearsal, a potential director walked in to look at what we were doing. He analysed what the song was about and what the dancing style looked like. While performing with my dancers in the rehearsal room, Ted's face, behind the director, was smiling with delight. He mouthed, 'This is the one!' to me. I performed as hard as I could and gave it everything I had. Blood, sweat, tears. There was silence once we had finished.

The director glanced up at Ted and spoke these words I will never forget, "I want to shoot this in the Philippines."

*

My life became absolutely crazy. I was less than eighteen and I was in the middle of planning my first video shoot... in the Philippines... under a label that I had been with for less than a year! Rehearsals became more and more frequent and my body seemed to ache all the time, yet there was nothing that I wanted more than to go out there performing and travelling the world. This was my dream, my passion, and it seemed to finally be coming to fruition.

My agreement with Ted was that I had to invest in half of everything that did not include large fees. This included all costumes, make-up, hair products and all the other necessities, like food and water for all the rehearsals. Many of these costs sound like fickle expenses that nobody would whine about. But trust me when I say that these expenses definitely added up. My mother and I began getting ourselves into debt. We did whatever we could to find the funds I needed knowing it would all be worth it to make my dream into a reality.

Sometimes, watching a three-minute music video, people don't realise that it actually takes such a long amount of time to create. Video clips can go from being planned for weeks, to months, or even years. My music video took three months... and everything was going to be fantastic.

This was going to be a huge spectacular. A large tank was going to be hired in the Philippines and we were going to shoot with massive lights and huge props. This was something I could not even imagine. It was more than I had ever dreamt it would be and I was super excited to go and start my journey overseas. We had discussed motorbikes, expensive cars and even the possibility of me flying in the air.

But clouds can pass over any blue sky and shadows can creep up at you at any time... You may think you're a star, you may think you shine brighter than everybody else, but that's just ego. Through this whole process, my ego was becoming more and more confident. Now my ego was about to be popped faster than somebody could even spell the word 'Philippines'.

*

One week before the big video shoot, I walked into the singing school early.

We (the crew: dancers, Ted's wife, the director and producer, and Coral's two daughters and I) were leaving in six days and my head had grown bigger than the peach in that kids' book *James and The Giant Peach*.

I was like the most spoilt and popular little brat at school, bragging to everyone about what I was doing and how famous I was about to become. I went from distancing myself in a depression-like state, having pushed my friends away during my previous sadness of not going to London, to becoming the loudest and most obnoxious person I had known.

Walking into school every day, I would drop into conversations and just start talking about myself.

"Oh, and we're going to have this huge tank painted in white, with me suspended in the air coming down in front of the camera, it's going to be incredible! I'm pretty sure, because it's in a tropical country, that we'll be able to have tropical animals like elephants and parrots! It's gonna be huge! I think it's going to be a hit over there as well! Also, the dancers' costumes are amazing... You should see us perform. I can't believe that I'm going to have my own dressing room... Can you seriously imagine how amazing that would be? No joke, we will probably have people outside taking photos, so we will need security and stuff, it's so stressful."

Deep down, I knew my friends and teachers were proud of me, but when something is great in your life, it is easy to forget that something stressful might be happening in somebody else's. Humility is key and modesty is totally underrated. It was not that nobody cared what I was doing, but they certainly didn't care to hear about it 24/7, everybody hated the way I was behaving. It was all about me. I had no time for anybody else and that's never a nice way to behave.

I was going to learn the hard way.

*

"What do you mean?" I heard Ted yell from the room next door. "How the fuck can you cancel an eleven person crew six days before they fucking leave? How can you pull out this money now?"

I was frozen in the hallway, my legs two heavy tree trunks, rooted, stuck and immovable.

"Fuck off!" he yelled.

I remember the sudden smashing as Ted threw his phone across the room, through the open door and out into the hallway, landing at my feet.

His wife, Rita, was crying and holding her arms up as if she had been hit. I had never seen this side of Ted before, but it didn't surprise me. Sharks tend to bite at some point.

Ted stormed out and Rita shepherded me to the steps outside the front of the building as she sat beside me while I cried. I cried from all the stress built up over the months and I cried for all the work that would come to nothing, I cried for everyone who was involved and how disappointed they'd be, but most of all, I cried for myself.

Even though there was an age gap between myself, Ted and Rita, they had become a combination of siblings and parents to me. All families go through hell, and I remember hugging Rita as she assured me that we would find another way to make this happen.

It's funny how in situations of dire trouble you turn to God and question his decisions. You ask yourself: What did I do deserve this? Why me? Why are you doing this? What have I done wrong? How is this happening?

But God rarely answers us directly and seldom simply hands you what you seek. Our life lessons are crafted specifically by his grace. They're fashioned to help us grow and develop into the people we will become. We often don't immediately see the value of these experiences. It's never easy. If it was, I don't think pride and a sense of accomplishment would even exist.

At my age, there was nothing I could do about it. I felt beaten and powerless. No money, no future.

*

The following day, I called Arianne to tell her exactly what was going on. I remember as she picked up the phone that I could hear yelling, screaming and the smashing plates in the background. In an ethnic family this could only mean one thing: that a huge fight was taking place.

"Hello, can you hear me?" I asked, as the screaming got louder.

"One second, I'm just going to go upstairs..." she replied.

The shouting became more muffled as she went upstairs. I pondered how I was going to tell her about all that had happened. Losing investors in any business means an almost dead end. In the music industry, it is very rare to find anyone willing to risk putting in money on a chance. The bottom line is everything. Statistics are vital.

"Sorry, dad cancelled his partnership with some guy yesterday... Everyone's always out to get money from him because we're well off. Sometimes he has to say no..."

I was floored. A different type of shadow, one I had not seen coming, descended quickly and enveloped me...

"Wh- wh- wh-what?" I stuttered, beginning to choke on my own saliva.

"Yeah, dad invested some money in this small music company, but he's backing out of the deal for some reason... I don't know. I can't keep up with all this business stuff, you know that."

"Oh-oh-oh, yeah, it must be h-h-ard to hear th-th-that all the t-t-time."

I couldn't help it, I began to cry.

"Are you ok?" Arianne asked.

It was funny how Arianne was even in the shadow of her own father. She was oblivious to the fact that his investment had been in my music career and that my life was about to go rapidly downhill.

Shadows and darkness threatened to engulf me.

*

The recording of Star Power's live taped auditions were underway and my email finally came through with all the details. They wanted me on the show! And in that moment, I was happy.

Through emails back and forth, they had decided to let me sing 'When Angels Cry' by The Duke. I was surprised that they didn't want the rock song they had asked me to sing, but went along with it anyway. I mean, after all that drama, I was back in business and ready to be on television again.

If they had liked the other song I performed better, then why would they ask me to sing the song that they did not prefer? I was a little worried and confused, but agreed nonetheless.

About a week before my next stage with Star Power, I received the email with an attachment to the instrumental of the track.

Ding.... ding-da ding.... di-di-di-di-di-da ding.

Absolutely not! This was a karaoke instrumental. It wasn't orchestral or sleek at all.

It sounded like something out of a Japanese karaoke bar that you would hear underneath inebriated people singing their hearts out to. Staggeringly drunk, more than a little worse for wear and thinking they sounded fantastic... the instrumental backing not helping their cause!

I had kept in contact with a few people since the first real, un-taped auditions and had contacted some of them to hear their instrumentals. Theirs were great. Every instrument sounded mastered and mixed perfectly. Every instrument in my instrumental was an electric keyboard version of some trashy late night tragedy.

I struggled to find a way out of the mess. My mind raced.

Once again, I was alone in the shadows; nobody was telling me anything and nobody was helping me.

At the time, I was not speaking to Ted as my decision to start this Star Power journey meant that I had broken my contract with his company. Since the blowout after the funding fell through, nothing related to his company was going anywhere and I didn't see him mustering up any possibilities of furthering my career. When I told him that I was leaving, he yelled and screamed and told me to get out of his life. His true nature finally revealed itself. I knew that I had to do what was best for me, but I was shocked at his ability to just cut me from his family, a family that had become my own. Abandoned is the only word I can use to describe how I felt at this point, but I had to do what was best for me. If people remained true to the things they said they were going to do, if people just did their jobs, none of this would have been a problem. We would have still been a family and had all the success in the world.

My job had been to sing and market myself, and I did just exactly that. What did Ted do? He hadn't secured anything and I obviously hadn't really meant a thing to him if he could drop me out of his life with just a few angry words.

After months of not speaking, I came to the conclusion that I actually needed Ted for one final request. I felt that it was the least that he could have done for me.

We had recorded a pop version of 'When Angels Cry' for fun, a couple of years prior, which had huge electronic sounds and an array of bass beats that would get anybody up on the dance floor. We had sped it up and given it a whole new dancehall feel. I decided I would ask him to borrow the instrumental we created. I knew it was a long shot, but I didn't have anybody else and thought that if he cared about me in the slightest, he would help me one last time for all the other times he had failed.

"What do you want?" Ted grunted down the line.

"I need the instrumental we did for 'When Angels Cry'," I told him.

"Whatever, I don't care, do what you want."

"Can I use it on the show?" I asked.

"Yeah, I'll sign it over to you, I want nothing to do with it if your name's on it."

Click.

My 'big brother' had cut me off and was treating me like a stranger.

*

I have this theory that if people care about you, that they'll accept your decisions, whether they like them or not. Ted may have believed I was making a mistake going on this show, but shouldn't family stick by your side no matter what? I cannot forget this crucial point: Ted and the crew at Purple Voices Singing Schools were not my real family.

Since leaving his amity and pursuing Star Power, the school in Sydney had branched away from Darryl Spade and created a new business name and a new business look. They were no longer the same people I knew. They were strangers.

If somebody pushes you into the shadows and somehow you allow this to happen, they can leave you there as long as they want.

After the track was finally sent over, I emailed Emerald, the music producer of Star Power who had been emailing me important information about the first live taping. I asked her if I would be able to use the updated instrumental and sing to that instead of the karaoke version they had given me.

To be honest, it felt like I was being set up from this point, but I was too excited about the prospect of being on television again that these thoughts only came into my mind in hindsight.

Emerald replied, telling me I had to get written rights from Ted as we had written the song together.

Now, any other day I would have thought this to be a problem, but from our brief conversation over the phone it seemed that Ted was eager to sign away everything. He wanted to get rid of me completely and he didn't care anymore.

I emailed Emerald back with the signed over rights to the track. I attached the necessary files and thought I was good to go.

How wrong could I be?

> *Actually, there's been a slight copyright issue so you'll have to sing what we gave you. See you next week. Emerald.*

*

At this point, there was nothing much I could do other than whinge and nag and moan to anyone and everyone that asked me how it was all going.

I wasn't going to make a fool out of myself on national television and it seemed like this was the producers' plan.

When you're placed in a shadow, it's very easy to get stuck in its darkness. But being forced to do something against my will... well, that's just not me. I wanted my instrumental, not theirs.

I sat and listened to the karaoke track over and over for about two days.

The original song had no rapping verses and our instructions were, because of copyright issues, to strictly follow the lyrics of the song.

Star Power in the UK had seen many contestants go on their show and rap their own lyrics and their own verses to countless songs that were even charting at the time. So I knew it was possible. I knew these 'copyright issues' were a load of bull.

Screw this crap! If Star Power are trying to push me, then they've succeeded. I'm gonna rap! I'm going to give it everything I have. They can't stop me.

I sat with a pen in hand and began to write my rap verses, calculating where the best rhyming words would go so they sat on the beat of the karaoke jam.

My mother's words rang into my mind over and over. Do the best with what you're given.

That's exactly what I was going to do. The best with what I was given.

Chapter Five

Mauled Without a Mask

Putting on a façade is easy. Animals do it: a chameleon will change its own colour to camouflage with its environment in order to remain safe. Spies do it: a spy conceals the facts, they never let the truth out and they never break character. Survival becomes an act. To act is to survive... Yet sometimes this protective mask is removed.

*

I've always found it easy to act. I mean, you act in music videos, on the sets of photo shoots and in meetings with managers and producers. My teenage years didn't exist for me. I went from being a child to an adult almost overnight. I would go to school with a smile on my face, wearing my mask, and I never let anybody know what was really going on... that home was not always the safe place you think it should be. Survival, it seemed, rested on my ability to act.

Emotionally, school was hard for me, and sometimes, keeping the mask in place was exceedingly draining, but on the outside I was everyone's best friend. People loved me, or loved to hate me. They saw me as over-ambitious or stuck up — a rudimentary 'wannabe.' But I knew that all my hard work would pay off one day. This wasn't something I was just doing for attention or self-praise. Many of my teachers and fellow students thought me a fool living in a cloud of make-believe. They wondered why I tried, thinking I wasn't even a good singer to start with and that I sure as hell wasn't ever going to be famous!

Unfortunately, lots of kids face abuse and this was, fundamentally, where my acting skills came from. And trust me, once you're an actor, it's very easy to tell if someone else is acting too.

Okay, let's face it, smacking your kids when they're naughty is normal. Of course I'm not saying it is normal for kids to get beat, but as previously mentioned, I'm not normal. Lots of parents will spank their kids lightly on the hand or give them a good smack on the bottom every once in a while. It's an old-fashioned kind of discipline that mostly doesn't do any harm. But things were different for me. I would come home from school most days to an overworked mother who was tired from working overtime trying to make ends meets, and a father who had been absent for most of my life. My father would enter the house full of rage because he hadn't made his daily sales quota—which he never did—and he would take it out on my mother, violently beating her. Somehow, the violence then trickled down to me.

When my father was finished, mum would be on the floor, bruised and bloodied. In my experience, at times like this, God leaves your soul. I'm sure Mum felt like she had no help in the world. There was no heaven in her eyes; no light in her heart. Perhaps He leaves to teach you a lesson, but what that lesson might be, I'm not sure. After a war of words and strikes with my father, my mother would turn her frustration on me. When it all got too much for her, I was her dumping ground.

There have been times where I have been dropped off to school with a run over foot, a messed up back and a jacked up face. I remember one morning, in a moment of thoughtless anger, my mother slammed her hand into my mouth, her ring cutting the edge of my lower lip. I firmly attached my mask and to everyone at school, it was just an allergic reaction to a bug bite.

These kinds of situations happened all the time. They became part of my daily procedures. My days often went like this...

* Get up at five thirty in the morning,

* Make breakfast and pack lunches for school for myself and my sister,

* Wake mum up from her wallowing heartache where sleep had been an escape,

* Get to school two hours early so mum could get to work on time,

* Be the most fun and positive kid in class,

* Listen to the end of day bell, take a deep breath and go home,

* Steel myself for the violence and watch the beating,

* Try not to think during the worst part of my day: get beat,

* Finally, try to sleep.

Now my personal life will, mostly, remain personal. But let me tell you, this experience helped shape how I understand myself. I know how to pretend. I can pretend to be okay. I can pretend that I'm not hurting and I can pretend to be strong. I guess I learnt that from my mother.

It's funny how you can forgive some things or some people and not others. I love my mother even though I know that she's one of the most messed up people you could ever meet. But I don't blame her. The way I see it, it's not her fault. Living with abuse for over twenty years must do that to a person. You forget how to stop the act, to stop the lie, and that's something I've always feared—forgetting how to stop the act. It is important to remember that sometimes everything is not okay. Sometimes it's perfectly fine to cry and sometimes it is vital to let someone else know what you are going through.

This hardly ever happened to me. I hardly ever spoke about my family life; I kept my mask firmly in place. I saved my tears for the shower or my pillow. They were no one else's to see. But sometimes, despite how hard you might try, you can't hide your pain. In these times, no amount of acting does you any good.

*

After the huge blowout with Arianne's father, Ted decided we would get serious and do things on our own. This was just before I decided to audition for the show, but before my falling out with Ted. Even after the money blowout, Ted had convinced me that we could still make it and I was still hooked on his fishing line. I still believed that even without the funding, Ted had my best interests at heart. I was obviously wrong, but at the time, I trusted him.

This time, we wisely started small, not biting off more than we could chew.

Deep inside, something told me this was going to be the last leg of our time together, (and thanks to Star Power it was), but as I said I'm a very good actor. Until I found something else, the next thing, something better than Ted was offering, I was going to remain enthusiastic.

"I've got a surprise for you," Ted announced to me one day at the school.

"What is it? Asian food for lunch?", I asked. I was hungry.

"No," he smiled, "I've booked you in at Studio Mambo to record Villain properly."

I was cautious, but ecstatic!

*

As Ted promised, we were to record our new single in a proper recording studio in the city. I say "we" because when I work with someone I believe it's a combination of effort. Yes, they're all my lyrics and ideas, but without help, you're nobody. I've always been grateful.

The night prior, I was prepped for my recording session: Ginger, lemon, honey and black tea in a hot white mug. The same ritual I used to prepare myself for the first taping of my Star Power journey. This time though, as I sat in bed prepping for the day to come, my father came in.

"Why do you have drink in your room?" he yelled.

"Dad, it's just tea. I'm drinking it for tomorrow…"

"What have I fucking said about food in your room?" He was fuming!

"But it's not food it's…" I was going to say 'it's tea', but I never got to finish my sentence.

Air. All I remember wanting was air.

My father strangled me. He slammed my skull into the tiled floor of my room. I didn't struggle, I didn't fight back. The message was clear: Do not take any form of liquid or food into your room again!

Recording was the next day and I didn't know what to do.

*

The night before Star Power was much different to the night before recording for the first time.

This time, nobody was going to hurt me. Nobody was going to negatively affect me. My mum had surprised me early on the eve of the audition with a five hundred dollar Jeremy Scott jacket—the same one that Rihanna had worn when taping her fashion show in the UK. I was so happy and so excited. I had my hair bleached, my teeth whitened and I was now ready for TV. Nothing was going to ruin this.

Before bed, I looked at my mask in the mirror.

Good. It was securely nailed to my face. Nothing was going to make it come off.

*

Daybreak shone its way into my window when I woke up at six to cover my bruises from the night before. I had been wearing make-up every day at school ever since I started to break out with zits. And it helped me hide the abuse I copped at home. No one knew and nobody noticed. In hindsight I guess that's why I have a knack for performance make up. I cover up what people don't wish to see, what I don't want witnessed. I concealed the bruises on my neck and face and made sure to wear a scarf just in case.

Ted was outside at seven thirty in the morning and we made our way into the city.

"Is everything okay?" he asked, knowing something was wrong.

"Everything's fine," I smiled.

As we pulled up at the large, silver-gated studio building, I could feel a loose screw in the mask I was wearing that day.

I was falling apart and the mask was coming off.

I just couldn't help it, I cried. Tears like never before poured out in Ted's car. The acting gig was up. It was too late to put the mask back on. I had been caught. I couldn't just pull myself together and leave the mask on this time. I was in physical pain. My throat hurt and I felt weak. I needed to cry.

As usual, this didn't stop me. I went into the studio and got the job done. I wasn't going to sleep it off like my mother. I'm not the type to feel sorry for myself. I could not change what had happened and in that moment I had to get over it and get the song recorded. At the end of the day it was still an opportunity for success...

The mask, although broken, had to be put on again. And that's what I did.

*

The difference between then and now is that now I am used to making sure that the mask never falls off.

A couple of weeks before Star Power's airing date, we received all the final information we needed to start filming the show. Scripts, final confirmation of karaoke instrumentals and things we needed to make sure we gave to the camera. I was truly shocked.

These television programs made out that everything was based on reality, but this was a lie, the whole thing was fake. We weren't the only ones wearing a mask. The whole show was a circus. The producers were the ringmasters. The production sets became a circus tent for all of us: Hair, make-up, stylists, food operators and more. They painted this 'reality', but this television show was the biggest illusion I had experienced.

On Kitty Kat Sundays, I had just been a kid... we were all kids. That show came with caring producers, apple juice boxes and ham sandwiches. No one was fake, no one was plastic, no one was transparent.

I eventually showed my family the Star Power scripts and karaoke instrumental I'd been given for my audition. They were also in total shock that I had such little freedom to show the real me, that I was being scripted to appear as the show wanted to present me.

"Don't you just sing what you want? Don't you just go up there and be yourself?"

I chuckled. No one has time to be him or herself in this business. You have to have a persona, an act, and luckily I had NOA.

The support I was left with after Ted ditched came from my friends and family. My friends bought tickets for the live audition show and my immediate family were all allowed to be filmed backstage with me.

I warned them all: Make sure you are all dressed in black. I had to look like I had a posse. Who you hang around with is a good indication of who you are. My family needed to match NOA's brand. Kind of like the Kardashians: chic and sophisticated. Masks on for everyone, a happy Australian family. If I wanted to be on TV, to actually be aired (because many get filmed, but are not 'TV worthy' and so are cut), I had to give the producers what they wanted: TV-worthy characters.

The producers had a clear direction for my family and myself from the beginning. I'm not flamboyant, I'm not gay and I'm not a diva, yet this is how they cast me, to be the stereotypical 'gay-diva', with attitude and sass, with an ethnic family who encouraged this loud and over-eccentric character. I had to give them what they wanted or my exposure on the show would have been cut to non-existent.

I can't tell you how much it annoys me that they cast gay people in this stereotypical way. In life, people come with a diverse range of personalities and characteristics, as well as their own sexual preferences. I hated that all this wonderful diversity was distilled into this singular image of being gay. After all, how do they know their 'Christina Aguilera sex-appeal clone' contestant wasn't a lesbian? And who cared if she was? But no, they had to ensure they would get ratings and planned to tick all the niche boxes to ensure that every possible 'group' was watching this circus act: gays, lesbians, country guys, divas, hometown girls, pretty boys, hipsters and rappers—you name it, if a stereotype existed, they would represent it on the show somehow in order to appeal to everyone and thus get the ratings they needed. They had contestants from different ethnicities, sexes and towns all over the country. Everyone had to watch. I was cast for the gay community.

*

We arrived at the arena two hours before the public. We were filmed lining up ready to audition.

They made it look like this was the first time we auditioned. Obviously this was not the case as we had previously gone through several filters and our numbers had already been culled.

They filmed each contestant walking up with their families and receiving a Star Power sticker with an audition number.

I stress again, this was not the first audition! They chose who they wanted to air. They chose who they wanted the public to see. After phone calls, further auditions and interviews, they selected who they wanted on the show. And even then, if you didn't deliver what was assigned to you, what was expected, you would be going home or simply not aired. They had total control of the show and the contestants.

It was also funny how nobody had seen the celebrity 'judges' yet. If they were meant to be judging us, wouldn't we have met them already, shouldn't they know us by now? Had seen us at least? Given us some advice? Judged us during our earlier rounds?

The mask of this show was getting more complex as each new layer was added.

Crowds, however, are something I absolutely love. Singing in front of seven thousand people was one of the biggest achievements I have ever experienced. This show was a huge platform to reveal to the public who I was and what I did. But if one mistake was made, it would have been the end.

The arena that we were in was one where countless famous singers had performed. I remember going to my first concert there at fifteen, alone with my friends and staring at the tiny singer on the stage from seats way up the back—we couldn't afford closer ones. I dreamt of being up there, of making a difference. Singing to the multitudes and impacting even one person's life. Here I was now, five years later and I was performing at that same place.

I closed my eyes before stepping out in front of everyone and put on the mask once again. Internally, I was freaking out. I could not give the show one thing to edit in their favour, not one thing that made me look bad and made them think I was 'cuttable'. The contracts we signed stated that at any point they could 'exploit' any footage they obtained during the show's production. If I made one error, they could edit and manipulate it in any way, shape or form. They could make me look like a complete imbecile. I couldn't give them any errors.

In hindsight it's funny how I could possibly have thought that no errors was even an option. There's always a way for them to cut your sentences in half, twisting what you've said so that it's revealed in a completely different context to the TV viewers. Trust me when I say, they are very good at editing...

I stepped into the spotlight and was ready.

The three celebrity judges were sitting at their panel as a production manager ran up and gave them all a few documents. The manager whispered something into their ears and then ran off.

Next to each other, the judges looked slightly comical. They were all singers from different genres, but didn't really visually or vocally match sitting next to one another.

Paul Ireland was an English singer from an old boy band that had been successful in the early nineties. He was the strictest judge on the show and had very strong opinions, which was ironic as he was one of the least successful of the three. He had grey short hair, slicked into a sort of swift comb over and was always in clothes that were way too tight. All the older women loved his sex appeal and he was notorious in the media for cheating on his wife and sleeping with contestants. I feared his opinion the most.

In the middle of the panel was probably the most success of all three judges. Purple Wing was fun, colourful and crazy. He was a designer and musician, but he couldn't sing two bars. His music was electronically digitised and he had club vibes in every track. It annoyed me that he was judging a competition based on vocal ability, when he never sang live, but out of all three he had sustained the most success and was internationally known. His songs were catchy, he appealed to a wide audience, and at the end of the day that's what matters. He was entertaining and foreign to us in Australia. Repping a huge purple afro, he was always in strange, galactic printed clothing and crazy, futuristic make-up: an intelligent gimmick.

The last judge was my favourite. A woman: for some reason I've always connected more with females. They have maternal instincts and to me, women are more caring. Writing that down I know how contradictory that seems. I see myself as very protective and maternally driven, even as a male, but perhaps it's because of my experiences with males in my life that I just find them to be hard to trust. Winona Waters was a famous Australian singer who found her own success in the shadow of her sister, Kate Waters. Her sister was on television shows in the eighties and broke out into a huge music career in Australia and the UK. Winona had followed her sister's footsteps and had recently made a name for herself in fashion. I admired her motherly nature and her sweet smile. She had short brown hair—but this changed every day as wigs were a prevalent part of her look—and she always wore short dresses and huge heels. In her forties, she was sexy and seductive and still looked like she could come clubbing with me and my friends on a Saturday night.

The three of the judges stared into my soul and I began to breathe heavily. As I held my microphone near my chest, I swear I could hear my heart beat through the speakers. How embarrassing!

Paul Ireland was first to speak to me. "So tell me about yourself, where are you from?"

Everywhere I looked were cameras and peoples' beady eyes.

"Umm... I'm NOA. I'm nineteen and I'm from Sydney."

"Nice, nice," replied Purple Wing, "I love Sydney!" he said, to rile up the crowd. Americans always played the 'I love Australia' card to get fans going. It was kind of annoying. How can you love Australia when you've made so much success in America, the music capital, and when America is your home?

"Tell me about your clothes, dude! What's going on, you look flash and cool and stuff. Tell me, what are you wearing?" he asked, with his thick New Yorker accent.

This is where I thought everything was going to go downhill. I did not know how to reply. I freaked out and literally made a goddamn fool out of myself.

I told him that one day I would be seen in leather and gold—which is what I was wearing then, my Jeremy Scott jacket and gold chains—and another day I would be in leopard print and ostrich fur....

Ostrich fur?

I don't know where that came from or why I said it. I've never owned ostrich fur... and they don't even have fur, they have feathers! I was a complete idiot. I was so nervous I was talking crap.

"Sometimes I wear checkered black and white with Scottish kilt print jackets and sometimes I'll wear Jeremy Scott teddy bear sneakers with my fur jacket, it all depends..."

"Not real fur?" he asked as the audience went dead silent.

I forgot he was vegan. Purple Wing was all about that hippie, spiritualistic and vegan lifestyle.

"Oh, yeah. Of course, fake fur! Fake chains, I'm all fake."

I actually wasn't. I was wearing designer and now I looked like I was wearing faux fashion brands. In the fashion world, this is considered to be a downright sin. You don't wear fakes.

"So why Star Power?" he asked with him arms crossed.

Everyone was staring like I was the comedy act, something for people to laugh at on the show. Maybe I was going to be there for ratings and entertainment. They were going to make me look like an idiot.

Answering his question, I put my hands up in defeat.

Gesturing and scanning my arms up and down on myself, I implied that I was here because I was fabulous. I was me, I was ready and I didn't care about this stupid chat I was having, nor the pre-recorded video-boxes I had been forced to sit through beforehand. These video-boxes were scripted video introductions that enabled the audience to gain an insight into who we 'really' were. They filmed me as I pretended to act sassy and dramatic, following their script, so I fell into what they thought a stereotypical gay guy was supposed to be. This introduction would draw in viewers before my audition started and would give people a little idea as to what I was going to perform.

I was here to sing.

"You're here because, just look at you, you're fabulous?" Purple Wing asked.

"Yes!"

"Do you think you can win this competition?" The audience fell quiet to hear my answer.

"Absolutely!"

As the karaoke music began to play I spat out rap lyrics faster than any other artist I knew.

The crowd, who had thought I was a joke, began roaring and screaming.

I will never forget that feeling. The thrum of the crowd was like a wave carrying me through the song.

As my voice began to project louder, the notes I began to sing just flew out effortlessly. Muscle memory: you practise it enough times and it just happens on its own.

To be honest, I don't even remember singing or concentrating on my performance. I had performed it so many times it was as though a robot filled in for me. I was on autopilot.

My thoughts were purely on the judges in front of me. I was also looking in the audience for my friends and family who had gotten tickets to see me.

As I scanned the celebrity judges' table, I noticed Winona's face change. We began an exchange of words, silently, in our minds.

'I really like your style, you're something really different. I don't need to be told

what to say with you. I don't need to read the script on my desk that the production manager left me. I don't believe your video-box. I genuinely and honestly just love what you're doing.' She winked.

'*Thanks*,' I smiled back.

At that point I knew I was through.

Magnifying Waldo

It seems to me that I have walked around with a permanent set of magnifying glasses strapped to my head since I was little. If we look closer into situations, we are often able to come to a better and clearer understanding of them. Unfortunately, some people are unable to look into the magnifying glass in this way, to witness what is *really* going on around them. I advise everyone to keep a pair of magnifying glasses in their pocket for when they need them, though it's true to say that even those wearing these glasses sometimes get surprised.

Magnifying a situation is actually easy to do. Just treat your life like a Where's Waldo book. Place a particular situation on repeat in your mind, like a re-run of a TV show—pun intended—and put your magnifying glasses on, ready to look closely and analyse.

The trick is to watch it over and over, again and again and again and again and again. Every time you watch it back, you pick up on something new that you hadn't noticed before or that you hadn't previously realised. Soon enough, you find Waldo.

*

To be honest I couldn't believe how I had pulled it off. I read the lines fed to me by the producers in my video-boxes and managed to get all of the celebrity judges to put me through. Or so I thought...

But by donning my magnifying glasses and rerunning the first live filming, I began to understand the show in much more detail. I saw that certain individuals were made to do things that others were not.

Contestants who were put through had received the most interview allotments with the green screen video-box producers. I was one of those contestants. We were filmed talking to our families and walking on our own; we were asked to do strange things like 'look worried into the camera' and 'anxiously await going on stage'. Star Power was a national television show. They needed ratings. They fed us lines they thought would boost those ratings.

The other contestants were included as a kind of 'background cast' so it looked fair to everyone else. Some contestants were only there to be filmed in small segments, their airtime was very minimal, but they could tell their friends and family to watch the show in case they were on TV. This meant more people watching the show. It also gave contestants hope to go and try again next year.

Out of all the contestants, only five per cent were actually even aired. The show's film crew spent more time with the contestants they had planned and wanted to air. These shows need certain stereotypes to appear every year so they typecast these contestants to fit into certain stereotyped roles: an ugly 'non-white' person with a great voice that they can transform and make up later, an eccentric gay guy with lots of sass, a young blonde girl who sings like Brittany Spears, a hot sexy girl group, a boy group who all have abs, a twelve year old with the voice of an angel, a young teenager who looks like a virgin with a double dose of oestrogen, and finally, someone, or a few people, with a really sad sob story.

These were the main stereotypes that the show would air. These were the people who the show believed would cause controversy, discussion and interest to TV viewers because they were all relatable to somebody.

When I place my magnifying glasses back on, I can see one of the producers handing Winona Waters a file with my face on it. Even before I got to that stage, they knew who NOA was, and who they wanted and expected him to be.

I remember Winona's response after I had finished singing.

"Everyone else has mugshots on their file! You look amazing! You're fabulous and I love the blonde hair!"

In a moment of heart racing adrenaline, those words seemed only like a compliment. But in hindsight, looking back over the situation with my magnifying glasses on, I wondered, '*What did she mean? What files? What mugshot?*'

I came to the conclusion that the files the producers were handing over to the celebrity judges were not files. They were prompted lines. They had already scripted exactly how each contestant's audition was going to play out. In reality, the celebrity judges weren't judges at all... they may as well have been actors.

I also remember how the producers would make me word things in strange ways. In my interview I said, "my inspirations are foreign artists from all over the globe. Artists that no one has really heard about, but in each of their own countries they are megastars: Medina, 2NE1, Natalia Kills, Aura Dione... I also like the mainstream Gaga and Nicki Minaj... I mean my creative side is like a love child of their two brands put together..."

I laughed. But the joke became a serious one liner after editing.

The joke became: "I'm the—love child of—Lady Gaga and Nicki Minaj."

They didn't care about me; they didn't care about what I said. They only cared about what would be good for ratings and so they cut my words and phrases and placed them together to create their own sentences that they deemed to be of better 'entertainment quality'. Hearing their edited line, the audience would have thought I was the sassiest, biggest egomaniac Australia had ever seen.

I also remember a young boy in the green room waiting to be filmed that day as well. At that point in time on that particular day, I didn't care about anyone else around me. I was working so hard to remain focused and connected to my upcoming performance that I wasn't even listening to my Mum when she asked me if I wanted something to eat. Examining now though, I recall this boy dancing around like an ostrich and pretending he was an Elvis impersonator. I thought he was absolutely terrible and had no talent in this business whatsoever. Yet as he stood there with his family, the producers were coaxing him to continue practising as they filmed.

This kid must have thought he was God, because there were four cameras on him and he was giving a performance of a lifetime backstage. But the cameras weren't on his side... He couldn't see that he was only there to be exploited for the episode's mockery audition.

The show had flown this boy's family out from Adelaide and had told him he was amazing. He had gone through the audition process like everyone else, but was told he was amazing: to everyone else it was clear that this was an utter lie. He signed the same exploitation contract we signed, so the show could do whatever they wanted to him. They were going to feed him delusions of grandeur until they could embarrass him in front of a live audience on national television; and that's exactly what they did.

He went up onstage to laughs, boos and a crowd hysterically crying out their amusement. This was not an audition. They had ushered him to a slaughterhouse.
*

This process of being stereotyped by the show was difficult too. It was hard having the nation see you as something you were not. I've struggled with people assuming I've been gay my whole life. I just didn't seem to fit the 'normal' image of a boy or male adolescent. It came to a point where I decided to question myself as well.

If everyone is calling me this, then I must be, right? Why are they shouting this label at me? If I'm gay, does that mean I act this way because of who I am?

Does acting a certain way constitute a sexual preference? My response is no.

All humans want happiness... and we all go looking for love.

Finding love can be like finding Waldo. We can find him on page three, yet totally miss out on page four. We can easily spot Waldo on page seven, but cannot find him on page nine despite how hard we look.

The show cast me as the token gay character and they stereotyped me as they wanted me to be. I played along because, principally, I needed the spotlight and that's the only role that they thought I could fill. It didn't matter that my vibrato was soft and smooth and my voice could go from melodic to angry rapping in five seconds. They only wanted the sassy song, with the sassy rap. It didn't matter that I could sport a three day beard and lumberjack shirt and look like every girl's dream guy; they wanted the sleek, made-up, fashionista show pony. It didn't matter how I defined myself or what my sexual preferences were. Little did the Star Power producers know or care that I was in an on and off relationship, with a girl, who I loved. We'd been together for five years and in this relationship I had dealt with my own insecurities of inadequacy and belittlement.

Lucky for me, I was comfortable to slip right in and behave how the show wanted me to. I was used to what society thought was gay: in fact, this how society mostly saw me anyway. Waldo himself, in society's eyes, probably looks gay: a striped outfit, matching scarf, matching beanie and glasses. He's not a geek. He's gay!

There's nothing wrong with being gay, straight or otherwise, but just because you're told you are something, doesn't mean you are that.

As a wise woman once said, sometimes you're 'Born This Way' and other times you choose to be whichever way you want to be. I may have been straight, but I was born with the freedom of choice. These choices do not define me. If I choose to wear matching stripes and eccentric jewellery, I can. It doesn't mean I'm gay, ugly, stupid or unfashionable. It's my personal freedom and my personal choice. And it should be everyone's.

My main issue with stereotyping is that some kids end up believing what they are told. If you put a child in a box, they just might find a way to fit that box; if you tell them the same thing over and over, they just might believe it of themselves. For me, this was a problem.

If someone is gay, this doesn't define who they are. We are not defined by our sexual preferences or the labels society gives us. If a girl likes soccer and athletic sports and wants to wear baseball caps, it doesn't mean she is or is not a lesbian, and it certainly doesn't mean she should be labelled as a lesbian. If a little boy wants to paint his room pink, it doesn't mean he is less of a boy or that he should be called gay. If a girl dresses promiscuously it doesn't mean that she'll behave that way, it simply means that on that day, this is how she felt like dressing. Who cares?

Children growing up should be able to make their own decisions about who they are and how they want to express themselves so that they can find their own sense of identity.

What really annoyed me about this typecasting was that the producers did not even care about anyone's feelings. Sure, I may be strong enough to keep singing and fight my way to the top, but this took a hell of a lot of strength and came with a lot of post-traumatic stress. I worried that some of the other kids would find it all too hard and simply never sing again. The pressure might have been way too much and the exploitation on live TV might be far too horrific for them to recover from.

*

The next few weeks of waiting for the next stage of the competition was quite nerve racking, to say the least. I had borrowed a large sum of money from family and decided it was time for a new wardrobe. I was going to be filmed over the course of a week and needed a new outfit for every day of that week.

My only forms of transport at the time were buses and trains as I did not have my license yet. I went with a couple of grand in my wallet straight to Sydney's inner city to start shopping for more designer clothes.

I sat on the train wondering how long it was going to be before my life changed. Before fame found me and I wouldn't be able to sit on a train again without being bombarded by fans or paparazzi. Little things like that may seem stupid to some people, but I have always been the type of person to take in each and every moment. Let's face it, no matter who you are, your life can change for the better or worse at any second.

I remember, as I was listening to my music as it drowned out the crowded train and receiving another email from the show:

Dear contestants,

Due to various network circumstances, not everybody who has made it to the next round of the competition will be moving further in the contest. You will be notified in the next couple of days with an email stating times and dates for the next round or an apology letter from the head producers at this network.

Star Power Team

I re-read the email over and over again.

You've got to be joking me. A major national television network and they didn't even have the money to take everyone they had promised to take through to the next round. I mean, it wasn't hard to work out that's what was going on. Purple Wing was paid almost a million dollars for his celebrity judge 'acting gig' and the show's ratings were slowly falling from those of the year prior. It looked as if the network had cut the show's funding and had hired in new judges to revamp the show. What they should have done was fairly and justly show more talent... but that's not how ratings work. 'Money over care' was clearly their motto.

I sat on that moving train and my thoughts completely changed.

Maybe I am going to just continue sitting here on this train, in this life that I have. It's not happening.

I hopped off at the next station and took another train straight back home.

*

As the train reached the last platform and I started walking up the stairs, I spotted Belle, the girl I had met at the very first auditions. It was like finding Waldo again.

She kept walking and the crowd kept shifting. I ran, puffing my way with my train ticket to be let out of the station's gates.

"Belle! Belle!" I yelled after her, running through the packed crowd.

She turned and smiled and made her way towards me as I fixed my shirt and my hair after my embarrassing public outcry. "Hey, NOA, how you doing?"

"I'm good," I puffed, leaning against the wall to catch my breath, "How did your audition go? Did you film your live audition? I didn't see you on the day I went."

Filmed auditions took place over three days in Sydney and three days in Melbourne.

How did people from Perth audition, you may wonder? From the first real auditions we all did months prior, the ones in other cities from outside Melbourne and

Sydney, were chosen to be flown out to act as if they had trekked there to audition.

"Umm, I didn't even get through to the lives, babe…" she said, slightly in embarrassment as her cheeks turned red.

"What do you mean?" I questioned.

She put her hands in her pocket in defeat. "They didn't call me back. My friend got through to the next round though, Vocal Discipline, next week… So I'm pretty sure this season is not for me."

"What's Vocal Discipline?" I shot back.

"The next round of the show. Where you have all these tasks and stuff… Didn't you get through your live show? I heard from my friend that you did. She told me this cute blonde guy who raps and sings got through, I assumed it was you?"

"Yeah, I did, but I just got an email saying I might not be…"

"What?"

"Yeah, some of us are getting cut regardless of us getting through…"

"Oh, yeah, they do that all the time. If you're a threat or if they can't afford it budget wise, they'll just tell you not to come in and you're off the show like it never happened. That happened to my friend last year."

"That's great…." I said in complete disappointment.

How was I going to tell everyone that I wasn't on the show anymore? How stupid was I going to look?

"Who's your friend who is through?" I asked, so at least I would know somebody if I did, miraculously, end up making it through.

"Oh, her name's Natalie. She's in a girl group called Senses. They're really cool." she told me.

"Oh, okay. Awesome…"

"Hey, I've got to run, but here's my number NOA, if you ever need anything, just give me a call. I have back-up singing rehearsals with Serenity so I don't want to be late."

Third time unlucky for her and it felt like it would be the first time unlucky for me.

I began walking home, listening to the old demo tracks I had written with Ted.

What was going to happen? I just didn't know.

*

Days passed and I heard nothing from the show. I was beginning to severely worry that my reputation as 'the one who always succeeds' was going to be ruined.

For me, succeeding had always been second nature. It's something that was drilled into me by my mother from a young age. My sister was allowed to flunk school, do what she wanted and just enjoy her time in class, having fun like any normal teenager. I envy her for that. That's not to say that my sister didn't try, but expectations of me were a lot higher. And I had high expectations of myself too.

From pre-school and kindergarten I was always vying for my teacher's attention.

"Who can tell me what colour this is?" Miss Sawyer would ask.

"ME, ME, ME, ME!" I would yell, practically breaking my arm, half standing-half sitting, so she would call my name so I could answer.

All my exam results had to be in the nineties and all my extra-curricular activities had to be something that I was the best at.

If someone was to stroll into my past and make their way into my classroom, they would see me answering every question the teacher was asking and finishing my work early to then go on to disrupt all the other students due to sheer boredom.

If someone was to stroll into my past and make their way into my dance classes, they would see me, front and centre of the routine, giving everything to my dance practice performance as if it was a concert.

I never did anything with half an effort. Ever. I gave everything my all! That was my problem.

Sometimes we show people amazing things and their expectations of us rise so high that we are no longer permitted to do anything wrong anymore; they expect perfection all the time. This is something I've struggled with all my life. We all have that crack in our personalities that is crowded somewhere amidst our every-day character. Who do we let see that? Can we let them see that? What if they do, if they see our flaws?

I remember being in grade three or four, just after Kitty Kat Sundays was filmed. Remembering how humble my mother wanted me to be, I kept my inclusion on this show to myself, my classmates were unaware of anything I had done. I remember wanting to tell them, to be popular so badly, to fit in. What I know now is that I actually was pretty popular all through my school life. I had many friends in many circles and everybody liked me. Just because you don't have the jock or queen-bitch status, doesn't mean you're not popular. Of course I didn't learn that until I actually became the queen bitch in high school, but nonetheless, I really just wanted to fit in.

One morning, as mum drove into the school car park drop off, the popular kids of the grade made their way from the corner store on their bicycles to the entrance of the school. I envied their freedom and made a comment to my mother about their allowances (that meant they could buy things from the shop each day). As usual, I got the same response: If you don't like it, live somewhere else.

I put my backpack on my shoulders and Sarah Gray, a friend in my class, rounded the corner of the school on her bike to meet with the others. Sarah wasn't in the popular group, but had started to talk to and befriend one of the high ranked girls of the group, Astrid Evergreen. Sarah skidded to a halt next to the group and I heard a ruckus of laughter.

Sarah had training wheels. Sarah was a joke.

You couldn't be in this popular group unless you could ride your own bike to and from school without help, and training wheels were seen as pathetic. After that, Sarah never rode her bike to school again.

I, however, did.

Just like Sarah, I did not know how to ride a bike. My father never taught me and I had only learnt to ride a Pee Wee motorbike with my cousin's help on our family farm.

After weeks of begging, my mother finally caved and bought me the Cycle5000. It was the shiniest bike in the world. Most of the kids in my grade had the Cycle 4.0. Mine was new and sleek. There was only one problem. I didn't know how to ride it and Mum had purchased it with training wheels.

I was not going to be Sarah Gray.

I decided to teach myself. Every night for about a week, I would wait for my parents to fall asleep so I could sneak out the back and take the Cycle5000 for a test run in the park next door. I stole my father's screwdriver from his workshop and decided to take cycling into my own hands. Nobody wanted to teach me, so I was going to teach myself.

Was I tired going to school every day? Absolutely. But the gratitude of knowing I taught myself was pretty fulfilling.

This is how I've grown up. Nobody is going to do anything for you if they don't get something out of it. When push comes to shove, you need to do things for yourself.

Needless to say, that Monday of the following week, I slotted into the popular group quite easily. I had convinced my Mum to let me ride to school, as long as she drove a few metres behind me.

My point here is that I've been expected to behave a certain way all of my life, and that's something I've put onto myself: the overachiever, the smart one, the successful one, and the perfect child. I wouldn't necessarily say it's a bad thing, but when something goes wrong, I don't know how to handle it. Do I get right up and keep fighting? Yes. Do I have a nervous breakdown before I get over it? Absolutely.

Sometimes I ask myself, 'Where's Waldo, NOA?' I then remember that he's taking off his bicycle training wheels. I've been doing this my whole life. Never stopping to relax. Always analysing with my magnifying glasses on, always thinking about what to conquer next.

*

I sat with my cousins Ellen and Crystal, watching our weekly viewing of Modern Family; my phone buzzed on the table near my Aunt Kathy.

"Thia [3], can you pass me my phone please?"

She passed over the phone and I saw that I had I received my email with information about the Vocal Discipline round of the show. It was in two days!

Three tasks where given to me via the email, with instructions and notes for what I had to prepare. Most of the other contestants had their instructions given to them weeks prior. I was a last minute add in for ratings. I guess they remembered I was good TV.

*

Shit. Waldo was going to have to work overtime on this one!

---

3 Hellenic word for Aunty

Chapter Seven

Gears and Motors

Life is full of streets and highways and tracks and paths; different roads that take us to different places. Some of these ways are nothing but overgrown tracks, filled with sharp vines, like the bushes in Snow White's forest, which cut and attack you as you attempt to pass through. Other paths, however, are a bright and harmonious to stroll down; a Mary Poppins-themed amusement park.

Humans are curious creatures, exploring whatever paths we find. And we always seem to be put in positions where we are tested or pushed to achieve: always aging and always accomplishing. We may go through rocky times, but we technically still learn and grow from our experiences—good or bad, we progress.

The road never ends. The race is never over. We are always tested. We are always being pushed to our limits. We are forced to be quicker, better, faster, smarter and more powerful. The car inside us speeds along highways and freeways, reaching new speeds and arriving at new destinations ever faster than before.

Sometimes we are pushed beyond our limits. We don't have to be physically tested or told to run a thousand-kilometre walk quicker than your average human to realise the outer reaches of our limitations, nor do we have to be mentally quizzed by astronomic and scientific maths equations that take days to decipher to know we are being tested.

Being emotionally tested is the worst kind of challenge.

*

After the email I received for the Vocal Discipline round of the show, I began packing my luggage with all my necessary outfits. I was to be there for a week. If I was kicked out early during this part of the competition, I would be sent home and eliminated. But something inside me told me I was going to be there right to the end. I had an outfit planned for each day.

The morning of this stage of the competition brought a feeling of accomplishment.

It was my time to test my own limits.

The email outlined everything we needed to prepare for that week. The Vocal Discipline round was split into three parts:

1) A cappella

2) Groups

3) Live Performance

I arrived at the competition and looked around as other contestants began arriving. Some of them I had seen in our live 'audition' and some of them from our earlier rounds that had not been aired on television.

Other than that, I did not know anyone, and regardless of those few familiar faces, I was alone.

The Moon Star Hotel was a huge complex in the centre of the city and had a vast number of facilities: short stay apartments, hotel rooms, function rooms and places where up-and-coming singers could perform shows to about five thousand people.

Singers with pink and blue hair were sitting in a corner of the foyer while the acoustic Indie singers with guitars were harmonising in the middle, near the entrance.

Not too long after everyone signed in, Star Power employees began assigning us to rooms.

They were putting our keys into the ignition of our cars and turning our engines on. This race was about to begin.

They sent us to our rooms and I noticed the 'better looking' contestants being sent up higher to the short stay apartments, whereas the average looking singers were sent to the overnight stay area in the lower levels of the hotel. It didn't mean much to me at the time, but as one of the employees handed me my room number, I realised I was on the top floor. I laugh as I write this now, but clearly they thought I was good looking.

We were asked to meet in the foyer fifteen minutes later, after we freshened up. There, the camera crew were waiting for us.

The crew ushered us outside and into buses that only fit about twenty people each. It was like herding cattle, the buses were overfilled and honestly, the average looking singers were left off the buses because of this overcapacity. I got on a bus.

Unlike me at the time, you may already have realised what was going on. At the time, all I was focusing on was our upcoming a cappella challenge and being filmed in the best light possible.

While on the bus, the Star Power crew started filming and asked us if we were excited and if we were ready to compete.

They had placed us meticulously on the bus so that they could get the best angles and the best shots. They were filming and focusing on about ten individuals. Making sure the lighting was good and the footage was usable.

We had been separated into categories and nobody was really paying me any attention. I was in the under-25-year-old boys' category. The other competitors all avoided me and I felt they were perhaps intimidated by my fashion sense and my confidence in talking to the camera. I've faced this kind of thing before. I've never had many guy friends, and the feeling of being alone was really sinking in. At the end of the day though, I was there for myself.

I listened to some of the boys' ridiculous responses. I felt like I was a black, sophisticated, customised Mini Cooper among a bunch of V8 Supercars. They were loud, obnoxious and had their motors revving on some serious fuel. But in my experience that's how a lot of guys behave.

I chose to look at it this way, the rare cars are the most valuable and that's why I was there. I was there to prove that even though I might be a pettier, sportier looking car, I could face the highway just as well, if not better, than the others.

I didn't have too long for all these thoughts though, shortly after getting on the bus, an assistant camera person was waving their hand in my face. He was pointing his finger at sign with a white X-shaped sticker on it that he was holding up. Of course I shouldn't have worried, I was one of the ten people they were focusing on.

"So NOA, how do you feel?" he asked, as the cameraman focused on my face and black glasses.

"Great, can't wait for tomorrow." I smiled.

"No, no, you need to respond with 'I FEEL'. Pretend we haven't asked you anything, we're just here to prompt you."

I remember thinking: *What the hell. I don't need prompting… If you want me to speak, I will.* They were trying to make it look like every other reality show out there: so realistic that it becomes fake. I mean, nobody is going to sit alone in a corner and talk to themselves about how they're feeling. Somebody obviously has to ask them something, or talk to them at least.

"Umm, sorry... I FEEL great, I can't wait for tomorrow."

They continued... "So how did you feel when you were being picked up from home... coming to The Moon Star Hotel?"

Picked up from home? Who was picked up from home? What a load of crack.

I looked up to the assistant who was gesturing me to answer anyway.

"Oh, I'm so excited, it was so good to just pack up and walk outside into this bus!"

It wasn't true, but I had to give them what they wanted. It was at this moment that I realised that the show had intentions all of their own, and not the intentions I thought. They weren't here to help fix my car. They weren't here to guide me to the right road. They were totally scheming mechanics, ready to send me down a dark and dangerous path, if and when it suited them.

*

After going nowhere, as we got off the buses, all of the categories of the competition were united, including the ones that had waited in the hotel foyer. I recognised a group of girls who had performed after me during my first live audition, so I went and stood next to them.

The camera crew began filming us walking into the lobby, with us pretending it was the first time we had entered the hotel. I wondered if any of viewers at home would realise we didn't have luggage; and speaking of luggage, I had two huge suit-cases, one full of jewellery, make-up and shoes and the other one full of clothes.

The producers of the show ushered us up onto a rooftop of the hotel where cameras were rigged all around us, some were on top of poles, some connected to bright lights.

Before we knew it, Paul Ireland, Purple Wing and Winona Waters came to greet us and give us our first challenge. Except we already had our first challenge, it had been given to us in the email...

"Contestants, we're so glad to see you once again!" Purple Wing called to us. "Congratulations on making it to the Vocal Discipline section of the competition."

Winona continued, "Finally it's time to hear your voices in a way we haven't heard th..."

"CUT..." someone called out. "Winona your hair is in the way of your back light camera! Can we have that again?"

The celebrity 'judges' were then ushered away and the whole thing was repeated again. Every mistake that was made by any one of them, meant two hundred of us standing there in the heat waiting again… repeating again… and again… and again.

"Tomorrow, you will all be singing a song, a cappella, to the three of us," announced Paul. "Pick a song that you identify with and show us your uniqueness and what you have to offer!"

This was quite ironic because the email we had been given with all of our challenges read:

"You MUST pick a song from the following titles: A, B, C, D or E. You may not alter or change the song in any form and it must have the same lyrics as the original material to avoid copyright issues."

How did these rules allow us to pick a song we identified with or to show our uniqueness?

It was hard to comprehend that what we were participating in was most definitely NOT live television. I wasn't stupid, I mean, I understood that everything had to be filmed correctly, but I was still under the impression that there was some truth behind everything, that there was still some aspect of reality, that the challenges were real, that the tasks were real… something!

It was like we were beginning a car race, but somebody had put an invisibility cloak around each of our vehicles. When the time was right, the producers would pull off the cloak from the vehicles they wanted to air on TV. It didn't matter who was the best driver or who got to the finish line first. And this wasn't the least of our concerns that night.

The producers of Star Power had decided to spice things up by wearing all of the cars down. They wanted to give us the wrong fuel for our engines, run us over tacks so our tyres went flat, send us down muddy tracks that dirtied up our sleek exteriors and make sure that we had used up all of the available petrol before our competition the next day.

Deciding it would be good for ratings, the producers had planned for Purple Wing to give us a debut of his brand new song. They made us wait a few hours before forcing us to be involved in filming with Purple Wing—he sang and performed while we all bounced up and down around him.

Wine glasses were being handed out to those over eighteen and cameras began to follow those lucky enough to be targeted with TV time. It wasn't long before I realised they were trying to get us drunk and make us tired so that we would screw up the next day and give them some ratings-worthy footage.

I refused to drink, I refused to bounce and I refused to scream.

"So NOA, what do you think of all the people drinking?" one of the assistants asked me, camera in my face.

Playing along, I responded, "This is a competition. If your priorities are alcohol and having a fun time, that's fine for you, but I'm off to bed to prepare for tomorrow..."

*

Sunrise crept through my window the next morning at about six. Luckily for me, I was in a room all by myself and had the luxury of warming up my voice without annoying anybody or being annoyed by someone else doing their own preparations.

I was cleaning my engine and making sure I was ready for the race ahead.

Adversely, I couldn't say the same for most of the other contestants. Many of them were hung-over, looked a mess and were just trying to keep it together. The producers were like those dodgy mechanics you hope you never encounter. They had purposefully tampered with our cars in preparation for their filming of the race ahead. They had left some cars brand new. Others they had irreparably damaged.

Hopping into my expensive leopard-print and gold tracksuit, I tied my bleach blonde hair into a bun and began putting my face on. I would make sure my car looked the best it possibly could. I needed to show the celebrity judges what I was capable of. Even if I didn't win this competition, I needed one of the judges to like me, to see something important in me in the hope that one of them would offer me a new opportunity. I mean, all of them were famous. They all had connections, and with connections come possibilities.

Back downstairs, the foyer was like a car yard of new and used cars: those who were affected by the night before and those who weren't.

*

New models of cars come out annually, as technology advances and style changes, improvements are inevitable. Humans also learn, grow and upgrade themselves every now and then. Some people choose to have the same car for forty years, always getting it shined or fixed, but never changing their models. Others buy a new car every year or so. But other than having the funds to do so, what is needed to upgrade continuously? When we look to change ourselves, attitude and personality are imperative.

I constantly change. I reflect and learn from my experiences and tell myself when, where and how I need to change. My car gets a new set of wheels, a new paint job and new rims with polished wax. I transform into somebody new: somebody with greater confidence and more knowledge.

You never know who you're going to meet on the road. There will always be people who give way and let you overtake them without an issue. There will be drivers who stop and help you out when you've forgotten the way home. Yet sometimes, you encounter drivers filled with road rage or you have an accident. That's just life, and hopefully you come through unscathed.

Sometimes we even have other people who come in and try to sell us a new model or a new way of thinking. That doesn't work for me, and the Star Power employees trying to force all of us to stay up late, drink and tire ourselves out was a perfect example. But they had met their match; I had been through it before.

I was about nine years old when my father wanted to change my car, literally. When I was growing up, my bed was a children's single bed in the shape of a red Ferrari. I never liked cars and never got into the whole automobile business like my father had. Yet my parents still tried to force me to be the image of a 'normal boy'. By this age, I was old enough to know what I wanted, what I liked, and to speak up for myself.

"Mum, I'm sick of this car bed," I complained, "I want a new bed."

As usual the response was, "ask your father."

My father, not knowing how to really connect with anybody under the age of twenty, decided to take it upon himself to 'redecorate' my room.

It was an ethnic, home, do-it-yourself project that ended up with two planks of wood painted with blue and white stripes: something that resembled the Greek flag. I had asked that they transform the bed into a dolphin, but obviously that creative direction had been either ignored or overlooked.

I remember walking into my room to see the car had been turned into this disastrous blue and white thing that I now had to sleep in. Crying wasn't an option. I was told to suck it up and respect the fact that an attempt was even made by my father.

That's how my engine works. You ask for something and if it doesn't turn out the way you want it, you suck it up until you can do something about it yourself.

The following week, I had nicely asked my grandfather to take me shopping. I desperately convinced myself that I needed a piggy bank to save up money. Entering the discount store, I saw just the thing I needed, a Sailor Moon moneybox!

Every day, the two dollars my mother gave me went straight into my bank.

After a few months, I had saved about three hundred dollars. I didn't hesitate in begging for a trip to the bed store. I wasn't happy with what I had been given, so I was going to get what I wanted on my own.

A few hours later, my new bed was assembled in my room; along with a matching tallboy that my grandparents bought me because they were proud of the responsibility I showed in saving.

A few months later I wanted a new desk and I was promptly told by my parents, "you can save and pay for it yourself."

Their expectations had kicked in. You prove yourself once, you show them your car can reach higher limits and then there's no turning back! Why would they buy me a desk when they knew I was now capable of buying it myself?

*

I anxiously waited for my turn to perform the first challenge. One of the producers on the show, Grace, walked up to me while I was practising.

"NOA, I know you emailed me regarding your song alteration..." she began.

The night prior, just after the staged alcohol fiesta, I had emailed Grace to ask her if I could change up my song choice for the next day. Remembering the task stated that we could 'not alter or change the song in any form and it must have the same lyrics as the original material to avoid copyright issues'.

I understood what I was asking, but being NOA, I needed another way to show my uniqueness and wasn't going to be put off by the rules we'd been presented with.

Her response that night had been, "Absolutely, that's fine."

What a relief... but today was a different story.

"Unfortunately," Grace told me, "I gave you the wrong response last night."

I felt a clenching in my gut. "What do you mean?" I questioned, nervously.

"It's your risk to take. If you want to change it up you may be disqualified, but you may be rewarded..."

Before I could ask her anything else, she ran off.

The producers knew I was capable of causing a dramatic scene for television. Sure enough, two minutes later, a camera crew with microphones made their way to my direction.

"So NOA, I heard you're taking a risk."

They were aware that my car was capable of reaching a speed limit higher than the rest of the cars in the lot. They were ready to exploit my engine. Push its limits. Just like my father had.

Chapter Eight

Pumpkin Soup

We create delicious and interesting dishes by using ingredients from all around the world. Chefs and cooks utilise a variety of foods to make traditional and outlandish meals in their restaurants. We all eat food; we cannot survive without it. Typically, as we grow up, our food is prepared for by loved ones, often our mothers or grandmothers.

Some people follow recipes, others have an innate and intuitive feel for food. Coming from a traditional background, my grandmother prided herself with her ability to master Greek cuisine. Although my mother's attempts were reasonable, they were nothing compared to my grandmother's meals.

Sometimes, following a recipe can get you in trouble. And leaving a pot on the stove for an extra twenty minutes can ruin your meal and destroy everything you've prepared, wasting the time you spent slaving away in the kitchen. I guess if you are the one who made the mistake, then it's your mess to deal with. Have you ever felt like you were an ingredient in someone else's experimental dish? What if someone used you in a recipe? What if they left you in the oven for too long? What if they decided to burn the meal, stuffing you in a boiling oven to slow roast you and burn you to a crisp?

*

After the producers discovered and calculated the risk I was about to take, they carefully constructed a beautiful television-worthy timeline to film for the show. I had playfully responded that I was going to take a risk and show the celebrity judges that I was bold and rebellious.

I was stuck together with the other competitors in a room all day, and we were only allowed to leave for lunch and dinner. The producers had the air conditioners in the room down to about ten degrees, hoping we would get sick and mess up. Everything was calculated, everything was planned.

They made us wait hours and hours until it was finally time for the girls to enter first and show the judges what she had to offer. Singing one out of the five available songs, a girl with pink long curls in an Asian-themed panda-style outfit made her way into the room. The whole day, this particular girl carried with her an expensive honey bottle and she kept squirting vocal spray into her mouth. She was sick when she arrived and was getting worse by the day due to the conditions we were in and the stress we were under. The producers were tiring us by forcing us to sit there for hours and giving us wake up calls at six in the morning. And we weren't actually performing until after four in the afternoon! Our rooms were upstairs and we weren't even allowed to go up and have a nap or freshen up.

I mean, I understand that it can be difficult organising this number of competitors and there is never enough people to chase after competitors who do the wrong thing, like stay out on breaks too long, but with everything that was going on, it was hard not to be the least bit cynical. Most of us had to sit on the floor, while those lucky enough to get in first had a chair for the day.

Fifteen minutes passed and the girl with the pink hair emerged, running out of the main filming room while the Star Power camera crew ran to follow her to get good footage. She was vomiting, coughing and sneezing simultaneously. She'd been pushed over the edge physically and emotionally, and the show got what they wanted. She had choked.

I imagined how she must have felt walking up onstage, in front of the celebrity judges, and have nothing come out of her mouth. This has been a recurring dream of mine almost since birth. Imagine standing in front of important people or a huge crowd, only for no voice to come out. Standing centre stage, already nervous, excited, and opening your mouth to a dry rasping sound... feeling a bit shaken, but determined and trying again... but still... nothing! Horror is the word that comes to mind.

As my category, the under twenty-five boys, were ushered into the filming room, my heart dropped to the pit of my stomach with nerves. I *was* going to take a risk. I *was* going to show them something different. If that meant that I was going to get eliminated, then so be it. One by one the celebrity judges called up our names to sing one of the five songs we were given, a cappella. Some performers were amazing, while others choked.

A young boy of about fourteen took to the stage and just stood there, frozen. Purple Wing and Winona were coaxing him to sing, while Paul just sat there unamused.

"Look, if he can't cope with the pressure, he shouldn't be here." Paul spat.

That was true. But I was nineteen, a whole five years older, and even for me the pressure had been like a knot in my stomach since I had gotten there. A fourteen year old simply wouldn't cope. He was too young, too inexperienced. And he hadn't grown up in this business like I had. Ninety percent of the people here had never experienced show business or the dark shadows of the industry. I feared this boy would be scarred forever and never sing again. It hurt me to know this, but I had to focus on the risk I was about to take.

My name was called and I stood up, my gold chains clattered together, making noise. From behind me I heard two of the boys in my category, Oscar and Tamar, snicker. Oscar was a country singer who had been on a similar television program the year prior. He hadn't succeeded. In his eyes, I was a joke. I was dressed unlike any other performer and he probably saw me as a comedic element to the show. Tamar next to him was a clone R&B singer who was a social media king. He was already famous online and the show had poached him off another program; these boys knew exactly how these shows worked and expected the worst from me. That was obviously their first big mistake.

I took to the stage as Winona, Paul and Purple Wing matched my face with pokerfaced glances.

"What will you be singing today, NOA?" Winona asked.

"A" I smiled, "with a little twist."

Silence enveloped the room. The group behind me gawked as I put my head down to calm my nerves for a second; Oscar and Tamar waited with sheer pleasure for me to screw up.

I began singing.

You shoot me down, but I'm not going anywhere,
I'm titanium, the strongest I've ever been...

The judges had heard this line a few times. Most of the contestants had picked this song out of the five choices. Yet no one did it like I was about to.

I paused. The judges leaned in.

Si si my, like Peruvian doors,
I'm waiting for all the competitors to jump on the floor,
And you be checking all the competition moving in hoards,
I'm like a matador chimin' in the brood for the call

I was rapping directly to them. No motherfucker behind me was going to outdo me! I wasn't going to let that happen. I looked behind as I kept free styling. Oscar and Tamar's faces were priceless!

It was risky to show them what I could do this so early on in the competition, but they needed to know I was a threat. And now they all did know, even the judges, and even the producers.

Everyone had cooked up a storm that day. But I was the crowning dish. My performance was the apocalypse.

*

Obviously after that performance I was through to the next round. That night they chopped up all the tiny celery sticks and threw the stems away—too bland! We were now down from a hundred and fifty contestants to just fifty. The pink haired girl was cut and so was that fourteen-year-old boy. A group of girls who I had begun talking to that day got through, along with a couple others I knew from my first audition day.

I walked into the verdict room and I swear Winona gave me a wink before they let us know our fate. Without any words being exchanged, I felt that Winona and I had a connection. It was like she had begun communicating with me with only her face. After the verdict she gave me a look that said, *Be prepared for tomorrow*. Prepared I was.

*

Always be prepared for the worst. If the water over-boils, your potatoes won't taste right. Your food will be a mess. What are you going to do about it? Buy McDonalds or try again? I had learnt this lesson from pumpkin soup.

Although this competition was something I hadn't experienced before, I had experienced circumstances that allowed me to have the strength to, as they say, soldier on.

Sometimes you're left to your own devices. When I was younger, my mother taught me that through her own experiences. One afternoon, she received news that my father had cheated on her once again. Distraught is definitely the choice word I would use for the situation. She had been through it all before, but I guess I was too young to remember much or understand what was going on back then. But at the age of ten, I was quite aware.

When my mother gets upset, she usually goes into overdrive. Domesticity becomes her passion. It's like if the only thing she can control is the cleanliness of the house, then she will control it to the max: cleaning, hoovering, mopping, cooking, dusting, polishing, washing, wiping...

On this particular day, she decided to make pumpkin soup. She knew that I liked the canned soup she used to give me when I was even younger. This time she wanted to make it from scratch. Perhaps she needed to achieve something, perhaps she wanted a little praise to boost her self-esteem, or perhaps it was her way of taking her mind off things. I minded my sister while mum went to the corner store and bought back fresh pumpkins that were bright orange. After a few hours of slaving in the kitchen, chopping, dicing, slicing, frying and boiling, the soup was ready.

She was just about to bowl the soup up for us when my father returned home. There was a heated exchange of words in the living room between the two. Nasty words were yelled from all corners of the house, bouncing off walls and into the kitchen where my sister and I were sitting as quietly and still as possible, waiting for dinner. I saw a glass bowl that we had in the living room smash over my mother's skull. My hands moved over my sister's ears and I started to hum to her to drown out the noise. She was petrified and the only thought in my head was that I had to protect her.

The yelling continued and more furniture was smashed before the war rolled out onto Wells Street. My sister and I continued to sit, the ruckus fading to silence between us.

After about half an hour, the front door slammed and my mother came in with a swollen face and a cut on her left eye. She smashed doors and slammed drawers in the kitchen, she splattered the pumpkin soup into two bowls and wacked them down for my sister and I.

"I made this for *YOU*, so you better like it!" she yelled.

I took my first slurp and almost threw up; it was disgusting. It was bland, rubbery and just downright gross. My sister made faces in her chair as well.

"You're going to eat it and you're going to like it!" Mum gave us little option.

"But Mum..." I muttered nervously, "I don't like it... It's not nice..."

She leaned down toward me, her face became like a monster's, her nose touching my nose. "You will eat it because if you don't, Dad is going to come and get you too..." she threatened.

My sister, Christine, started crying and my mum whisked herself away to the bathroom.

Christine looked at me as if begging me to eat the soup. She didn't want to get hit. She was also the victim of this dysfunctional home and she was young and scared. It was the first time I think she actually understood what was going on. I had tried to keep her from a lot of things and cover stuff up for her, but unfortunately, the level of domestic violence was too much for me to hide.

I sat in my chair prepared to eat. I ate my bowl in futile, difficult attempts. Every spoonful was like eating dirt, but I finished mine and ate my sister's as well. Neither one of us wanted the wrath of my father that my mother had threatened us with.

In the end, I vomited.

My mother came out of the bathroom, took one quick look and called me a prick.

I sat in my own vomit for about an hour before being beaten and then cleaned up. I was shocked beyond belief and too scared to do anything.

No one on the show knew where I had come from, but I told them I was prepared for anything.

*

After we had been given our verdict, I trotted out of the verdict room with confidence. Everybody was staring at me like I was a god. They had underestimated my abilities. They had no idea I was Colonel Sanders' secret KFC recipe; these bitches were just unseasoned chicken boiled in flavourless water.

I felt all eyes on me as I walked through the corridor to the lift to my room. I was the star here, the main ingredient in the fake pot of this façade of a show. Without me, the show would soon descend into boredom and, suddenly, after only one performance, they all knew this too.

As I reached the door to my room—a guy with blue hair who I had noticed on the first day I arrived—stopped me to pat my shoulder. "Hey, I just want to let you know that I thought you were really great today…"

Amidst all the stress, it was nice to hear something positive from somebody.

"Thanks," I beamed at him, and I walked into my room to get some rest for the next day.

*

As usual we had to set our alarms for six o'clock in the morning; the producers were determined to tire us out.

Today was the only challenge in our paperwork for the Vocal Discipline rounds that we did not know anything about. We didn't know what was going on or what was going to happen. We waited about two hours for production to get their acts together and made our way into the foyer where producers were giving us our task.

Purple Wing came in for about five minutes allows the producers could film him giving us instructions. Apparently they were going to put us into groups and give us a group task.

This was definitely a recipe for disaster.

The groups were being called out and put together: all the gospel singers in one group, country singers in another, Britney Spears look-alikes in another... you get the idea.

Left over was a combination of eccentric singers who did not necessarily fit any of the usual moulds that society tries to fit them into.

The boy with the blue hair was left, I was left, this Mexican singer named Kelly was left, a dancer with a high pitch Mariah Carey voice was left, an urban rapper who couldn't sing was left, this older woman who was a female version of Purple Wing was left and this boy who looked like Justin Bieber but who had a Ne-Yo voice was also left. We didn't fit into moulds, so the producers decided to chuck us in together, random ingredients into one big melting pot, and make us sing none other than Lady Gaga's 'Telephone'.

We were all unique and different in our own way. I wouldn't say everyone in this eclectic group were all great singers, but they all did bring something unique and different to the table. It was like taking Asian cabbage, Spanish onion, a meat pie, German frankfurts and a piece of tiramisu and trying to make one cohesive and tasty dish out of it. It was headed for disaster. We were all too idiosyncratic, too independent, too different, and too self-absorbed to harmonise together. We all thought we were stars and were all very different.

I figured that the producers needed to kick some of us off. They only had room for one 'different' type of singer in the finals: the wildcard.

This is where things took an obvious turn for the worst.

They stuck us with a vocal coach who was giving out singing parts. Collectively, we had agreed on what we were singing already, but we headed over to the vocal coach to get his opinion anyway.

"No, NOA, you'll be doing a rap in verse three and Dylan (the boy with the blue hair) will be doing the high Beyoncé part," the coach instructed us.

"But I can't..." began Dylan, butting in as he knew his vocal register wouldn't go that high.

"Well, Dylan, you're going to have to figure something out," demanded the coach.

I stood there confused. I wanted to show them that I could really sing in this round and they were trying to pass me off to be just a rapper.

I shouldn't have been too upset, I mean, at least I knew I could sing in this style, but there was already a rapper who couldn't sing in this pot of vegetables. I didn't want to be associated with him.

Practising all day, we tried to dance and sing together and work out some kind of cohesive routine. They didn't tell us when we would be performing, so we tried our best to come up with something good in the first half hour.

Before long, screaming, yelling and fighting broke out between Kelly and the high-pitched Mariah singer. The other rapper was rapping over the top of them and they couldn't hear each other's harmonies. I added my ten cents by telling the rapper to wait for his cue because he had timing issues. Dylan decided to keep trying to hit the high note he'd been given, which only resulted in a wail and an off-sounding alarm noise coming out of his mouth. It was chaos.

The heat had been turned up. The water was simmering and whatever stew the producers wanted to make from us was coming to a boil.

"Guys!" I snapped, totally frustrated, "Get it together."

As I yelled, I saw a camera creeping over Kelly's head with a microphone underneath my legs being moved with a handle rod by one of the producers.

Great. They just got me yelling on film!

Ignoring that matter, I took the lead and guided the group into rehearsing without any further arguing.

About two hours later, we were sent to a choreographer who gave us all new moves that we had to waste time learning. We had already organised what we were doing, nobody had told us we were going to have to work with a choreographer. Once again, they decided not to tell us, they decided to let us waste precious singing rehearsal time coming up with our own moves, only to have that swept aside by the choreographer.

After more waiting, it was time to go in and film this second part of the Vocal Discipline competition round. We could hear the gospel group practising and they sounded amazing. This was obviously a set up. They had been given Emily Sande's song 'Next To Me', a typical gospel anthem, and were all amazingly tuned together harmoniously. Their voices were like chocolate melting in your mouth: perfect and irresistible. Our song sounded like Shrek and Donkey singing together on a drunken ride home from a magical nightclub. We were doomed.

Our turn approached and we got into our allocated positions. The three judges didn't even appear to be too bothered with us at this point. The only one who seemed to admire our time and efforts was Winona, who I'm sure smiled at me as I entered. Purple Wing looked high, he was munching on gummy bears while he sat on the panel, and Paul wasn't paying any real attention, he was on his phone! They were paid to sit and watch, but in reality, they didn't care. It was the directors and head producers who sat behind them in the dark who were waiting to judge the lot of us. I began to realise that they were the ones who were making all the decisions.

"Alright guys, we've put you all together because you're all different and unique. We're expecting something special and marvellous!" Winona warned, just before we started.

After her cue, the music began playing and it was show time.

As I thought, the rapper missed his cue, the Ne-Yo Bieber kid almost fell off the platform we were given to stand on, and the two young girls in the group were yelling louder than one another just to competitively prove who would be deemed a better singer by the judges. Dylan with the blue hair did not hit his note with any greatness and my part was coming up next.

I was in a group that was literally and spectacularly failing. We could have been amazing, but nobody had worked together. So I thought, stuff them! It was not my job to save the group. I needed to save myself.

I banged out another original rap, impromptu, on the spot, while singing between pause lines. I wanted to show them both my singing and rapping abilities and I didn't care that my whole group had just screwed up. I walked into the middle of the platform and made the stage my own. If I didn't fit as part of the meal that was being cooked, then the judges were going to get a good side dish, that's for sure.

Instead of allowing the others to retake their turns, I kept singing and rapping right at the front while they all knocked into each other. Here and there, I let the Mariah Carey singer named Jessie have a moment singing on top of me because I realised, while rapping, her voice blended well with mine. Other than that, this was my game to win.

The song finished just like those comedy movies where two people battle it out and at the end, stepping in front of one another to be the only star in the spotlight. The judging panel was not amused.

"I'm going to say two things," remarked Paul. He paused, "...Some of you rose to the occasion..."

Winona looked at my direction and gave me a beaming smile. It could have just been my own perception, but in her mind she was telling me that I had done a good job. I loved our secret connection—whether this was real or not, I needed the reassurance.

Yes I know. I killed it.

"Others..." Paul continued, "Attempted things they shouldn't have."

He looked at Dylan.

Yet how was this Dylan's fault? He knew he couldn't sing that part and had asked for another. Technically, being put in this crazy group was nobody's fault either. We all attempted to do things that would see us through to the next rounds, but were stuck with a fair few limitations.

"You are dismissed," Paul said, ushering us out of the filming room.

Walking out, we were met by the host of the show who began asking me questions about how well I thought we had done as a group.

"I think we all tried our best. As Paul said, some of us did rise to the occasion and pull it out, while others did sink a little bit, but overall, effort was made by everybody and I think we did the best job we could do under the circumstances..."

I've learnt to never rat anybody out in this business. I wasn't going to name names. Every singer there was having their heart broken, and I wasn't going to add to that more than was necessary. Every person there had a family and friends who would hate me if I said something negative. So that wasn't going to happen.

As I was asked more questions, I noticed a producer stick a whiteboard up with the words: NOA? GAGA? Written across it.

"So did you enjoy singing a Lady Gaga song? You like Lady Gaga don't you?"

This irritated me a lot. Just because I dressed a certain way didn't mean I was automatically a Lady Gaga fan. I didn't sing her song for my initial audition and I didn't tell anyone I liked her.

"To be honest, I don't care if Lady Gaga liked our rendition or not. I like her music and I think she's done an amazing job in the industry. She's made room for other individuals to be unique and progress with music. I did enjoy the performance, but that's all it was... A task we were given and we did our best."

The producer rolled his eyes and called, "CUT!"

Yes, I did like Lady Gaga, but that had nothing to do with my performance. Did they want me to say, "Yeah, I think we ultimately destroyed one of the biggest popstar's multi-platinum singles, live on television?"

No. I'm not as dumb as they thought. They'd have to try harder than that to bait me.

The dishes they had mashed out of us were over. We were a disgusting dinner/dessert that would give anyone who ate us food poisoning. Luckily for me, I was the only nice part of the meal.

Chapter Nine

The Scent of Roses

When we use our senses, when we become aware of the world around us and we open ourselves to triggers. We may see something or hear a noise or a word that triggers a long forgotten memory. This may be a fun loving memory: every time I smell burnt raisin toast I recall the Saturdays when I was about nine that me and my mother used to eat breakfast together while my sister was dancing ballet. We would go to a diner near my sister's dance school and have the most awesome breakfast ever. The toast was cut really thick and my mother taught me how to dip my toast in my coffee, which I still do today. Because of her, the toast tasted better.

Yet sometimes the memories that are triggered have a ghastly after-effect in our brains. They bring into clear focus visions of things we may have wanted to ignore, at best, or at the very least have wanted to blur into obscurity.

*

While we waited for our verdict, the producers of the show decided it would be fun to humiliate Dylan for his inability to sing the part of the song that they gave to him in the first place, the part he knew he could not sing, but that they had insisted on. The cameras flared around him like flames from which he couldn't escape.

"So Dylan, do you think you ruined a song by your favourite popstar? Did you let down your community?" The cameras zoomed in for a close-up.

What community were they referring to exactly? Dylan dressed a particular way and yes, was gay. Were they referring to the 'gay community'? What the hell did that have to do with anything and why were they bringing a specific group of people into this situation?

It was bad enough they tried to pull this kind of stuff on me. But I was different: I was older and I was straight. Lady Gaga, in my eyes, didn't symbolise a sibyl, taking a stand for the LGBT community. I saw Lady Gaga as an inspiration to musicianship and to the abilities of unique singers. Dylan was out and gay and, as any human being should be, was proud to be who he was. As far as I could tell, Lady Gaga had helped Dylan, and many others, shine in the shadows that the majority of the public had cast onto them for so many years: as they had done to me in the past. From what I know, she is not just a supporter of gay rights, she supports individuality and promotes individuals being true to themselves. This is an idea that I agree with and a message I also strongly endorse.

I didn't know why they were pulling this card on Dylan. Was it to embarrass him? To stereotype the gay community? To remind everyone that if you're feminine and have blue hair that you will be viewed as gay? To mock everything Lady Gaga had done for this community and to test the reactions of this community when she was brought up? Or did they do this simply to create controversy in the hope of increasing viewer numbers and the show's popularity? I didn't really know what they were doing, but it pissed me off.

Dylan stared back at them blankly, with a naïve, puppy-dog faced look.

"Dylan? You auditioned with a Lady Gaga song... How do you feel now that the judges think you butchered a classic?"

I saw his eyes begin to tear up and it triggered in me the memory of a time where I was put on the spot in just the same way.

When someone interrogates my integrity or questions who I am, I go ballistic. The producers had purposefully just crafted a way to make it seem like Dylan had just let down the whole LGBT community over a song they made him sing and a part they made him perform. He didn't choose any of this and the fact that they were basically taunting him about his sexuality in order to get a reaction out of him, really triggered my nerves.

*

I had just turned eighteen when I told my Uncle to go and fuck himself.

Ever since I was a small child he had been questioning my whole existence as a human being, questioning my whole life. If there is one thing that I absolutely despise in this world it is questioning somebody for who they are by stereotyping someone's characteristics and their behavior.

My uncle hated the fact that I had a naturally gentle nature. I began dancing at the age of four, and had practised singing ever since I could talk. To my uncle, this could only mean one thing: that I was gay.

You see, stereotypes really piss me off. I cannot stand how somebody, another human being, can try and box somebody else into some type of category for behaving or acting in a particular fashion. Everybody is his or her own individual and everybody is unique. Stereotyping is done by those who lack the understanding of those who possess 'atypical' individual traits; who lack the compassion and empathy needed to accept people for who they are: uniquely amazing individuals.

My uncle had been annoyed at me my whole life due to the fact that I had never played soccer or joined in athletic sports. He was the soccer coach to a quite successful junior soccer league in the area. He added the word faggot to his vocabulary when I was around. The fact that I didn't play soccer, to him, meant that I was undoubtedly gay. While this was not the case (I was and always have been straight) I had to deal with his harsh, torturous words for over ten years. It was at the age of eighteen that I decided enough was enough.

I may be so defensive about stereotypes and boxes because I have struggled my whole life with this idea of generalisations and I have fought against being pigeon-holed. Growing up in an ethnic family, it was seen as disrespectful to speak to an adult 'out of line'. I had held my tongue for years, unable to stand up for myself or defend my integrity. It was after I turned eighteen that I decided to call him out for being such a homophobe and such an absolute asshole in front of everyone. To me, turning eighteen meant that I was an adult and could now express my own opinion, like my elder cousins did.

That Christmas, after I had just turned eighteen, my uncle stared at me, deep in the eyes, and started his usual rant about my supposed inability to be masculine. I decided to give him a taste of his own medicine, which was quite ironic because his daughter was there and she was in fact a doctor.

I turned to him and I explained to him how, at eighteen years old, I had already begun recording an album, was working three jobs and had no interest in beginning to play football or soccer. I then proceeded to explain to him that running around in short shorts and high-fiving men playing with balls on a dirty field was not something I was interested in. In my eyes, slapping each other on the arse after scoring a goal was more of a homosexual act than singing into a microphone. While I don't think there is anything wrong with physical contact between men, I knew it would get a rise out of him to make him think that he had participated in an act that he thought was taboo. Twisting his idea of a friendly act between men and turning it into a homosexual encounter meant that he was just as gay as he was trying to portray me as being. Challenging his views made me feel exultant. People like my uncle, who don't understand individuality and can't see their own skewed perceptions, find anything feminine in a male to be 'proof' of homosexuality. So I, being the villain, decided it was time for me to volte-face the conversation and give him a taste of his own medicine.

"Go fuck yourself," I said to him, "I have absolutely no interest in hearing what you have to say from this point onwards."

Enough was enough.

*

I stepped in front of Dylan and turned to the firing squad that faced him. In my head, I had put on a fire fighter uniform. No flame was going to hurt either of us.

"You don't have to make people cry. If they cry naturally, like that girl did yesterday, then go, run wild with your little cameras. You don't have to keep tricking people and forcing them to humiliate themselves on television!"

At that point, I kind of knew that my time at this competition was coming to a close. Things between the producers and I were becoming too confrontational. I wasn't giving in to their carefully crafted verbal traps anymore. Furthermore, I could see what they were trying to do to all of us and I had no interest in humouring them.

I defied what they wanted. They wanted somebody to comply with all their little games, invisible rules and ridiculous regulations. They wanted a robot. They wanted to make sure everyone participated in their amusing ways to create what they thought was good television: embarrassing yourself in front of a million people.

I knew I wasn't going to do that, and I wasn't going to let them do that to this poor kid either.

The camera crew walked away, eyebrows raised in shock as if they had been so severely disrespected. It was clear they had an attitude of disdain for all the professional competitors who came to the show and had their own opinions. Having your own opinion was apparently a crime here.

"Thanks, NOA," Dylan sighed.

"Anytime."

*

We all received our verdict that night.

By a miraculous turn of events, I had made it to the final round of the Vocal

Discipline section. Unsurprisingly, Dylan did not. As expected, every other 'unique' person was eliminated. The producers kept Kelly and the Mariah wannabe and made them form into a duo for ratings. They figured the fighting between these two would be fantastic for viewers.

How would Queen A and Queen B get along?

They had kicked off any other person who was different in order to showcase the two girls and me alone. They couldn't have any other performer who was different and unique on the show at this stage. Otherwise, too many people would ask why, when these amazingly talented individuals were kicked off. The producers needed to kick them off early to eliminate the risk of any of these performers coming up with anything good later on; that's why they shoved us all together, to create disaster from which they would choose and keep their golden ones.

When I made my way back to the waiting room, the girl group, Senses, who I had made friends with, were sitting on one of the couches the show had brought in for us. Only now that we were the last top forty contestants left on the show did we get couches. Were we all meant to feel blessed now that we actually had furniture to sit on?

We began talking and I noticed a small camera a few metres away pointed in our direction. We laughed and joked as we discussed how we were being watched now from every angle.

Our conversation intensified and I laughed, bringing up how the camera had no microphone to record our conversations.

"There's probably one under the couch," I joked.

Out of pure amusement and curiosity, one of the girls, Natalie, who was friends with Belle who I'd met at my first audition, decided to look underneath the couch. We all cracked up laughing, but lo and behold. There was a huge filming microphone taped underneath the sofa.

Shit.

Our talking ceased immediately and I began speaking in Greek to one of the girls in the group who was also of Greek descent.

"Don't say another word. Tell the girls too. They're watching us and they know that we know their games now. Play it very safe and don't do anything wrong. Do you understand me?"

She nodded and whispered our revelation to the others. It was a strange thing, knowing what was under that chair.

I've always had a problem with looking underneath couches and chairs. It brings back a disturbing memory.

When I was about four or five, before my father lost his money, my family had been quite wealthy and lived sumptuously.

There was one room in our house that my mother had named the Toy Room. It was on the outside of my father's office, and that's where my sister and I would play. We had a reclining couch in that room that folded out into a bed for visitors.

I hate that couch.

I recall the moment when I first realised that something else was going on in my home, just like I realised there was something going on during my time at the show. Ironically, in both instances, my realisations came from under furniture.

My parents were screaming about something, and this was the first time I understood what it meant to be unprotected. My father had thrown a glass at my mother and had gone into a heinous rampage, knocking everything over in sight.

When I realised what was going on I slammed the Toy Room door shut and turned on the radio to hide the noise from myself and my sister. I honestly can't remember what song was on because I was too distracted with trying to avert my sister's attention, but I do recall that I was crying while attempting to divert her.

A banging on the Toy Room door came next. My father wanted to get to his study and the only way to it was through the Toy Room. But something came over me and I wouldn't let him in. I placed my sister in her bouncer chair and turned her to the wall so she wouldn't see anything.

The next moment, the Toy Room door flew open and my mother rushed in to save my sister, leaving me unprotected.

The boxing match had started with my mother, but after he was finished with her, he decided it was my turn. I was very little in size when I was younger and I managed to use this to my advantage. With superhuman agility, I manoeuvred my way to the first place that I thought would hide me and shelter me. The recliner.

I slithered my way underneath the recliner to where my father's arm could not fit. All I could see were the springs of the mattress underneath and the rose coloured pattern that adorned the mattress. Looking back, there's something quite prescient about the rose pattern on that couch. The word rose actually has Germanic origins and once meant 'fame' or 'famous' back in older times. I'd like to think that at the darkest points in my life, God presents himself as a reminder of who I am and who I am capable of becoming.

As I scurried under the recliner, monstrous hands and fingers tore underneath it, to the back of its corner where I was hiding. My father wanted to grab me and pull me out from under it. If he succeeded, I would be finished. I could only guess what he was capable of doing. To this day I still hold traces of resentment towards my mother for not protecting me. As a mother, I feel it should be your duty to protect all of your children. I also believe that the word mother is a very strong word. You don't need to be male or female to be a mother. I know I am a mother figure to many friends and to my sister. Being a mother means becoming responsible for the ultimate protection of your babies. I was left under the couch alone.

I stuck my back, curled up to the nearest corner of the couch and sat in the foetal position, waiting for it to be over. The yells were thunderous and I didn't understand why my mother had not come to try to grab me too, to save me from him, to protect me.

All I could smell was the couch. I can't describe it, nor do I want to. Every time I smell that scent, to this day, I almost hurl. It takes me back to that place and, after we figured out what the show was doing, I swear that same scent was in the air. I struggled to maintain my composure.

*

We were down to the final ten from each category: ten groups, ten boys, ten girls and ten over thirties.

While most of the finalists had been instructed on the final challenge several weeks prior to filming, we were filmed as having only 'one day' to prepare for our final song in this part of the competition. Understanding now what was going on, I already felt defeated.

It wasn't like I was going to give up at any point—I'm not like that—yet I just didn't see the point in this whole thing anymore. Coming from a performance world at a young age, I just thought there would be some authenticity here: a type of real measurement of talent.

The producers walked around each day with our name highlighted in red or green. Green meant we were staying, red meant we were going home. The producers knew exactly who was headed home from the competition and when they were leaving. They knew who they wanted in and who was going to be in the top live shows of the competition. It was all planned and all figured out. There really wasn't any point in competing.

I remember going downstairs the day before the final performance and saying goodbye to Dylan and the rest of the people who had been kicked off from our disturbing group performance. Looking closer at their plane tickets and train tickets home, I saw that they had been purchased one month prior to the date they were leaving.

How could the producers have known how well the competitors were going to sing in the competition? Why were all the plane tickets booked and dated one month ago? Could this mean that the finalists were already selected?

Everything started to make sense. The people who were going to make it were in the highest suites of the hotel; where I was. The rest of them were in the smaller rooms in the lower levels of the building, and their tickets to go home were waiting, already prepared for them. The whole competition was orchestrated.

I was over it all.

*

There's a famous Shakespearean quote about the smell of roses. You can name a rose anything you want, but at the end of the day, its smell will still remain lovely and, despite what you might call it, it is still a rose. My interpretation of this means that if you can smell bullshit, it doesn't really matter where it comes from or what you name it either. It's still a load of crap. This show had a terrible stench to it now, worse even than the smell you sniff when you're driving behind a sewerage truck.

After we were sent back into our rooms, I rang my mother...

"Mum, I think I'm going home."

Chapter Ten

The Holy Tongue

Sometimes it's hard to convince yourself that somebody is watching over you and that you're being protected. So many times we go through our day to day lives thinking about nothing but the day itself and the activities we are putting our minds to. We actively and subconsciously forget to be thankful: to thank God for the day we have been given and for the health and love we have in our lives. I've been raised in the Greek Orthodox faith—a very strict Christian sect of Catholicism that ties in Greek traditions and Hellenic historical conventions. My grandparents, also of this faith, taught me that God is almighty and that He will answer any prayers that are strongly enough evoked. I remember attending church one Easter and reading the Bible out loud in Greek with all the other church-goers to prove to my grandmother that I was the better grandchild and that I was faithful to the Lord. In my family, if you respect the Lord, you acquire more respect from others.

Personally, I describe faith as a candle. There comes a time where a candle burns and turns to wax, extinguishing the flame as the last part of dry wax melts and envelops its string. Candles can be used over and over again, you just need to relight them. Just like wax, the flame of faith can be ignited, over and over again.

The last night that I was on the show, I prayed all night. I begged somebody to give me strength where I couldn't seem to find it myself. Somehow, over my teenage years, I had lost God and didn't really know where to find my faith again. There have been three instances where I have. One was when my father slammed my skull into a tiled floor and I knew that some higher being was protecting me. The second was in the hotel room on my last night at the competition and the third I will get to soon.

*

The night before my final performance, I decided to have some Manuka honey mixed with chamomile and garlic. A special mix I use to make sure my voice is in working order.

I v-logged (video logged) my experience that day, as I had been doing since I arrived, on my personal webcam, crouched on the floor next to my bed.

God, it's me. I really need your help now and I don't know how I'm going to get through tomorrow. I'm aware that something is going on and I don't know what that is. Please give me the strength and courage to stand and remain strong during this experience.

I've always been quite intuitive, ever since I was very young. It was at this time that I looked up to the heavens and sought protection from the Lord, my angels and from my loved ones who were looking down on me. I needed to remain strong and keep fighting as long as I was there.

*

On my sixteenth birthday, my immediate family gathered at my aunt's house to have a family dinner, a tradition that we still keep to this day on all important occasions. We were all in the kitchen: my aunty, my mother, my two cousins, Ellen and Crystal, my sister Christine and myself. Discussing everyday business, we went back and forth through conversation, laughing about old stories and letting each other in on the latest family gossip. Out of nowhere, one of my cousins decided to make a comment about a sibling that wasn't in the room.

"Do you remember NOA's twin?"

Excuse me?

"Yeah, don't you remember that conversation?"

"No, I don't what are you talking about?" I said, stunned.

"Your twin that died..."

"What twin that died?" I asked.

My mother has never been a good liar and turned to me chiming in, "Yeah, don't you remember?" She paused, "I told you a couple of years ago about your twin?"

I had never been told about this sibling, and I had absolutely no idea what was going on. In a strange way though, I felt my birthday was probably not the best time for this information to have been brought up. Yet there was nothing I could do about it. Sitting at the table eating that night, I felt completely uncomfortable. I had been sitting for the last sixteen years on a lie that I hadn't even known had existed.

When we got home that night, I asked my mother to explain what the hell was going on. She proceeded to explain an absolutely horrific story. She began the story by reminding me that this had all happened a very long time ago.

When she had been in the middle of her pregnancy with me, my father had decided that he did not wish my mother to keep the baby. But by the middle of a pregnancy, it is absolutely impossible to make a decision like that. Even if a woman decided she wanted an abortion at the halfway point of her pregnancy, she is too far along for doctors to undertake the procedure. Halfway along is already past the point of no return. But my father was adamant; he did not want a child, and kept insisting.

My father's way of achieving what he wants in the family has always been to become violent. He decided the best way to get rid of the child was to abuse my mother physically to the point that she would 'accidentally' lose the baby.

One night, while she was going down the stairs, he took it upon himself to push her, and she tumbled helplessly down the staircase. At this point she was unaware that she was carrying twins and thought she had lost her first and only child. An hour after her fall, there was blood on the floor and my mother did, in fact, realise that she was no longer carrying. In recent years, I've learnt that this was not the only pregnancy during which my mother suffered abuse at my father's hand and which resulted in the loss of an unborn child. More recently I discovered that she was forced to abort another child after the birth of my sister, due to my father 'having enough fucked up children already.'

The image still turns over and over in my brain: I picture my mother being hurled down the stairs pregnant with me, and apparently a brother I will never know. This image that I've never seen this with my own eyes, is somehow an image that I will never be able to erase from my mind.

The show had just as many secrets and skeletons as my parents did and I didn't like it one bit.

After the incident, my mother had called my aunty (her only sister) and was then rushed to the emergency room where they told her that she had definitely lost the baby and she would need to see a doctor the next day to get everything, as my mother explained, 'cleaned out'. This term that my mother used, 'cleaned out', really affected me. To this day I'm not really sure what they do after something like this happens, but I can only imagine how horrific it must be for a mother to go through.

The following day, the doctor gave my mother an ultrasound; while analysing, he paused for several seconds and then zoomed in on the black and green screen in front of them both.

"You still have a child in there," he said.

Both my aunty and mother looked up in a state of shock and confusion.

"You've only lost one. You need to calm down so your body doesn't shock your baby or you will lose this one too." The doctor told her, "Go home and rest so you don't hurt your little boy."

As my mother continued to tell me the story, I stared deep into her eyes in complete shock. I was a miracle baby! My whole life I'd had the feeling that someone was looking over me. Now I knew who that someone was: my twin, a brother.

In a strange way it all made sense to me. I had always felt protected and always felt like something was taking care of me throughout my life. I had never been completely harassed or bullied at school to the point where I couldn't handle it. I've had several near death experiences, which most of us have probably had before. Once was almost drowning in a pool and the other was parasailing at school camp unharnessed. On both occasions, I had been protected and left without a scar and without catastrophe! During these moments I have always felt as if it was not my time to go and that somebody had definitely looked out for me. I can now say that I definitely know that this had been my brother.

Staring at the ceiling as I said my prayer, I hoped that my brother would hear my call and protect me from the storm that was coming the next day.

*

I woke up the morning of the last day of the Vocal Discipline round with a feeling of distress running through my body. A knock on my door alerted me that the day of filming had already started.

"So NOA, are you excited to perform tonight?" The questions began.

"Yeah, I can't wait," I lied.

I knew something wasn't right. I could feel it in my soul. I guess it was times like these where I actually felt like my brother was with me and everything all made sense.

I had a custom-made jacket that I had been saving for a special occasion. If I was going home, I was going home with a bang.

I wore a black and white leather varsity jacket with my pseudonym 'NOA' on the front of the left breast pocket. The word 'VILLAIN' was adorned across the whole back of the jacket. That day, I embodied that word, and I still do today. If the producers wanted to play games, I would give them the best game they had ever played.

I went downstairs to the main foyer where the contestants were standing. There was now only twenty four of us left. Six in each category and two contestants had to go.

What really irritated me about that whole situation was the fact that the public wasn't witnessing any of this. This was all pre-recorded and the producers would later edit out anything they didn't like or that didn't fit their agenda for the show. They wouldn't show me talking about perseverance or hard work and passion for music. All they wanted to show about me was the image of a diva who made sassy remarks. If I was going home, then I was going to be aired the way I wanted so I wouldn't look like a complete idiot when they were done with me.

The array of cameras and microphones were ever-present that day. There was one producer-camerawoman whom I had grown quite fond of while I was there. She was actually the woman who allowed me to see the verdict every day before it was announced to us contestants. She would leave the paper on one of the speakers near the auditorium we were filming in and give me a wink. The contestants who were through were the ones highlighted in green, and the ones in red were out, eliminated and about to head home. Her name was Marcella.

The only people I had to lean on were Natalie and her girl group, Senses, and a girl named Riff who was an African American, Beyoncé-style diva who I admired and had started to talk to the day before.

Senses and I became really close during the competition. Maybe it was the fact that we were all ethnic, I'm not sure, but we really held a strong connection to what we were doing and where we were coming from. In the space of two weeks, we had formed alliances and friendships that one might form after years. We were closed together in a weird environment and had become quite tight-knit.

That morning, I received a phone call from Drita and Maja and told them that there would be seats for them in the audience. That night was a performance in front of a live audience, unlike what we had seen in the other rounds. My family was yet again coming to watch, and it was really lovely to have the people who I loved there beside me to support me. I guess in some weird way, I did not want to let them down. At the end of the day, if I became super famous, it was all for them.

We were sent to work with vocal coaches that the show had brought in that day.

Little did we know that the coaches were writing notes and analysing our vocal abilities to run to the producers and let them know whether we would be good candidates for the future show episodes to be aired on live television.

As usual, I didn't miss a beat. I could hear the coach whispering to one of the producers (my luck, it was Marcella) and, after a few minutes, I was told I could go to my dressing room to get ready for the final round of Vocal Discipline. If I made it through, I would be going overseas to be mentored by a famous overseas celebrity.

I had always wanted to travel with my career and it was unfortunate that I had not had the opportunity, after I signed with Ted, and had remained here in Sydney.

It would be such a fantastic opportunity to be able to go overseas and experience a music world where I would feel at home, and an environment in which I would feel a sense of achievement. I looked up to the ceiling while getting ready and prayed to God that everything would be okay.

Of course, being who I was, I had forgotten a gold necklace at home and ordered my mum to go and get it for me, ignoring the fact that this was an hour drive for her. The mission it took to get this necklace was ridiculous, but I needed God with me and that necklace was the gold cross that I had been baptised with. I needed His support and guidance.

To add to the day's struggle, I had been allocated a Michael Jackson song to sing. You think that was the worst of it? It absolutely was not. Another two boys were asked to sing the same song. Now, I'm not good at maths, but if you have six boys and four spots available, it means you've given half of them the same song. The producers had already picked out three performers to go to the next round, and the three remaining would battle it out with the same song to get that fourth spot. Did they think we wouldn't figure this out? I mean how dumb did these people think I was? What worried me more was how naïve everyone else seemed to be. I talked to Natalie, but she didn't seem to have a clue what was going on. The average person, apparently, was so oblivious to everything, and that really was frustrating!

Once again, just like my first audition, I was given karaoke music, and Oscar and Tamar (the boys who had snickered during my first performance), were in the clear. Oscar was allowed to sing whatever he wanted, I mean they had poached him from social media and the kid already had over twenty thousand followers, so they needed to keep him to keep the show's ratings up. Tamar was singing the same song as me, but had been allowed to use a guitar to sing with. If that wasn't a set up, I don't know what was.

I wasn't going anywhere without a fight. How could they compare us boys together? Two of the boys were classical gospel singers and Omar was an R&B mogul. Tamar and the last boy were country singers, and I was Pop and Rap. It didn't make any sense to me—how could they compare us?

*

Believe it or not, when I was younger, I knew most of the Bible parables that I had heard in church. My grandparents were very religious and, for whatever reason, I always had to try to be the favourite child, so I immersed my head in the Bible each night, reading and learning. I recall reading everything and anything when I was younger, but I made sure to read my religious novel for my grandmother. Every time I would visit her, I would stand tall and recite a parable. I would be given a red twenty-dollars to go into my money bank. My grandmother has always loved me and wanted me to splurge on something I wanted to buy, knowing I was still saving my money for a rainy day.

In the predicament I was in now, I remembered a line from the Bible about tongues. They saw what seemed to be tongues of fire that separated and came to rest on each of them. All of them were filled with the Holy Spirit and began to speak in other tongues as the Spirit enabled them.

To this day, I truly believe my brother spoke through me and brought this parable into my mind at that time, but I will obviously never know that one hundred per cent. The parable explained that after the resurrection, the Holy Spirit gave the apostles the ability to speak in tongues and languages to spread the word of Jesus.

I knew that a rap was what the song needed. I needed to spit those rap verses like tongues of fire and let everybody know what the hell was going on. I began writing to the karaoke music they gave me. Rapping in a Michael Jackson song was risky, but I needed to take the risk. I needed to expose the hypocrisy of the show, but I couldn't just start rapping about them conning everyone. I had to write in tongues and metaphors.

I stood on the stage with my family and friends present in the audience. I didn't care about the judges or producers. By that time, I was there to make a point. I sang the song and stopped as the music finished.

Then... I began rapping without music, alone, standing there with my message.

Wanna kiss you but my future is loser, won't stop till its super don't call me at all,

Need to get down on your knees, pretty please, won't be thieving, I'm plead-
ing with you on all fours,
Nasty I see y'all are cleaning your paws, after destroy us you sounding the
snore,
Need a big trick, a magician just came to illusion the way onto heavenly doors.

Those who had the lights turned on would know what I was saying.

I sang my story and received a standing ovation from the whole six-thousand-person audience.

But what happened next was sickening.

Chapter Eleven

Leeches for Light

Brains are like light bulbs. Holding the capacity to spark up at any point with the heat of electricity, they are able to spark up with an idea that resonates through our minds. Sometimes, we are able to spark up our own light bulbs, but at other times, we need a little help from other avenues.

The most violent form of illuminating a light bulb is when the electricity that has sparked it doesn't belong there or is a higher voltage than the bulb can handle. When external forces spark you up with an idea you never thought possible, this can be a fantastically collaborative moment. But if the intention of others is selfish or hurtful... I advise you to run.

*

The final night of the Vocal Discipline round saw me celebrating with the girl group, Senses. I had become quite close to Natalie, in a platonic way, and was invited to their room down the hallway.

I don't know what told me that I was going home, I just had a gut feeling that my time in the competition was over, especially after my hostile admonishment to the camera crew. Why sit and mope around about it when there was nothing more I could do? I had just received a standing ovation and if I was eliminated now, most people, in Sydney at least, would now know my name. It was time to celebrate this.

After bidding farewell my friends and family, who had snuck in to see me perform, I made my way to the vanity room in my suite to freshen up and then went to meet Natalie and the girls in their room.

The electrical charge I received walking into their suite was not what I expected. As soon as I walked into their suite I felt a feeling of anger and resentment that I had never dreamed of possessing. I hadn't previously known it was possible to feel so much anger and frustration simultaneously. This electric shock that shot into me was too much pressure for my light bulb. It was going to explode. I could feel it. I was going to explode.

As I opened the door, I saw a party was happening, people were singing and music was playing on some radio speakers. There were about twenty people in the room, excluding the girls and myself. Some faces were recognisable, unfortunately.

"Come have a drink, my little boy," said Natalie, lifting a glass of something alcoholic.

"Er... No thanks." I muttered.

The recognisable faces belonged to some of the producers of the show. Why were they here exactly, partying with the girls?

As I was introduced to more and more people, I found myself in a room of connected wires. Circuits that traced back many years with many identifiable associations to them. One of the contestants, Jake, who was still in the competition, had his vocal coach with him in the room. The vocal coach was a member of a boy band, called Four, who had been runners up in the competition the year prior when Serenity Hayes had won. The leader of this group, whose name was Fido, sat on one side of the room chatting to one of the producers. I concentrated hard, listening to their conversation and learnt that this boy band had recently signed to the record label associated with each year's winners from the show. They had found and poached for the show, Jake and Danielle, the Asian girl who the show was focusing much of its time on. As far as I was concerned, this was yet more evidence that the show was all pre-planned and pre-meditated. I was also confused about how Natalie knew them.

"NOA, meet my manager Fido..." Natalie interrupted my thoughts.

You have to be fucking joking!

Was this even a competition or a family pep rally? I could not believe the connections these people had and how duplicitous the whole show was. How could the show not be rigged when there were producers partying with contestants outside shooting hours? How could the show not be rigged when people, like Jake, were given free passes to be here and had not been through any other audition process thus far? He didn't have to lie to his mother and sneak out of the house to audition like I had; he had been automatically put forward.

I felt like throwing up. I didn't like what I was hearing or seeing.

"Nice to meet you, Fido... Natalie, I'm going to go back to my room, I'm sorry, I'm not feeling that well and I need to prepare for tomorrow's verdict. I'll talk to you guys later, it was nice meeting you."

I didn't make a scene, I politely made my excuses and left the social gathering.

My light bulb had overheated and was blown into a million pieces. I had no energy left.

All I can remember after that is vomiting in the bathroom out of utter shock and disgust, before crawling into bed.

*

Unbeknownst to the producers, I had calculated how their system of getting rid of contestants functioned. The morning rounds of paperwork were given to the camera people and videographers with our names highlighted to indicate who was going through and who was going home. Our value had been screened and tested with a record label in cohorts with the competition and they had already made their choice about who would win. The whole show revolved around this and manipulated the audience to believe this was a fair and just competition. Any bystander watching the taping of this show would agree that it was centring on the Asian girl named Danielle, framing her story around her 'incredible voice' and 'ethnic struggle'. They let her do whatever she wanted and she was filmed twice as much as any other contestant. It was basically reverse racism by the whole media, but I don't want to delve into politics here.

*

The final day of the Vocal Discipline round had arrived and I was woken up by Marcella, the producer I had grown fond of during my stay there. She came into my room to let me know that, as far as she knew, I was safe in the competition, that she knew how stressed out I had been and not to worry. I found this very comforting and was able to breathe a little easier for the rest of that day. She told me that the runner had come early in the morning to drop off their run sheet for the day with all the information they needed. At one in the afternoon, my verdict would be filmed and I would be free to go at around two. I thanked her for her support and then she asked to film some 'getting ready' shots in my hotel room. Of course I agreed, she had been so nice to me, how could I not?

Walking into the waiting room that day was very different from any other in the competition. I no longer felt a sense of family or belonging with any one of the other contestants, especially after what I had seen the night before. Everyone was in on things, everyone was working their own secret agendas and I didn't feel comfortable anymore. They say that in a short period of time, people who wouldn't even glance at one another twice in real life can become the closest of friends when placed in a small environment together—seven days straight, sixteen hours a day. The bond that I shared with most of these people was slowly diminishing. I no longer felt related to them because I realised I had nothing to relate to. I might be ambitious, but I wasn't a cheat. I wasn't working any angle other than my own performance talents. I wasn't part of any of the secrets I had discovered.

We waited around for hours for filming to begin again. During the other rounds, our start time had been about eight in the morning, with everyone awake at six ready to tire us out so we would be exhausted by the time we performed. We had usually performed just after noon, but pre-recorded our personal segments and video-boxes during the morning.

On this final day of the Vocal Discipline round though, things were quite different and we all were very baffled. It was already four in the afternoon and we had been waiting in the room for about eight hours. Danielle had filmed about four video-boxes while the rest of us had filmed two. Jake, the boy with the manager, was allowed rests, snacks and breaks because he was under sixteen and being so young he was given privileges due to child laws that none of the rest of us got to experience. I would have loved a nap and some time to rest, especially after last night.

The other seven of us who were left in the under 25 boys' category were kept on standby for about two hours. Standby means that you're not able to go to the bathroom, eat, sit or do anything. All I remember was that I was busting to go to the bathroom. After another half hour, we were told to head back to the waiting room.

All remaining categories of the competition, girls and groups, were exhausted at this point. We really didn't know what was going on and thought perhaps that something major must have happened to one of the judges. As you, dear reader, may have guessed by the way this story has been going so far, this was not the case.

Out of the blue, a runner came around and began handing out new sheets of papers to all of the camera crew and video producers.

"Fuck off," I heard one of them say.

"This is bullshit!" Another yelled, "How the hell...?"

We, each of us competitors, all stared at each other, confused as to what was going on. We looked from one to the other, our own confusion mirrored in each of our faces.

"Nuh, I'm not doing this shit anymore," yelled Marcella, loud enough for the head producers to hear her and she threw down her earpiece, "I didn't sign up for this!" She walked away, tearing the paper that had been given to her, leaving her camera crew unattended.

As she walked away I saw her turn in my direction and mouth the words: *I'm sorry!*
*

Ideas can be good or bad. Catch the right idea and it can allow us to prosper. As a young boy, I remember thinking if I sang loud enough in shopping centres that somebody in a suit would be the talent agent who would discover me. No one put this idea in my head; it was an idea I had created all on my own.

But the world isn't that simple. It turns out that some ideas are intangible and are only dreams. The light bulb only shines when dreams and thoughts collide and create something magical. A dream on its own, is just a dream. On occasion, darkness follows your light, ready to suck you dry. Darkness usually waits for the perfect moment, when your light bulb is shining at its brightest, before cutting it off. Just like that, darkness takes your energy, your power, your dreams and ideas. When I explain how the light works, I usually compare it to Tinker Bell—the fairy. The more that the world believes in the existence of fairies, the more Tinker Bell will shine, brighter and brighter; the more people who support and encourage you, the more confident you will become. However, there is darkness in this world that doesn't believe in your ideas and your brightness. I call anyone who promotes this darkness a leech. These leeches latch onto your light and suck every part of your gleaming brilliance to keep it for themselves, destroying you in the process. Some of these bloodsuckers take your light to use it against you, killing your optimism completely.

I remember auditioning for Star Power at the age of fourteen, five years prior to returning this time around. I didn't even make it to the staircase of judgement. Can you believe that they actually called me a 'fat wannabe'? I had the idea back then to try my luck at fame and show the world I could sing. I was only fourteen and they called me all the names you would expect to hear come out of a bully's mouth and not from the producers of a show who were supposedly there to foster great talent. They extinguished my light and tore me to pieces in the space of two seconds. But that hadn't hurt as much as what was happening this time around.

It hurts more when the darkness allows your light to shine brighter and *then* cuts your electricity supply. It's like the shadows befriend you, deceive you, and kind of wait for you to be at your strongest before proving to you that you can't keep shining. That no matter what you do, darkness still exists to vanquish the light that you have.

*

I didn't know what Marcella's *sorry* meant, but I knew that it probably wasn't good news. I looked behind me and saw the shadows descending as the darkness began to envelop me.

"Alright guys, it is time for your final verdict."

We marched through the doors into the filming room where the celebrity judges stood in formation.

They called out the winners who were entering the final segment of the competition, which was the live performance rounds to be aired live on television.

They didn't call out my name and they didn't explain why. Just like that, the darkness struck.

At each stage of the competition, there had been an explanation as to why those who were eliminated were not going through to the next round. Even though these explanations were bogus, unhelpful tokens, at least there had still been some form of explanation given by the judges to confirm that our elimination held some kind of validity. These explanations were also created so that the public would believe one of us had faltered or had made a mistake and, therefore, had to leave.

This time there was no explanation; no reason.

I guess in a weird way, I'm glad there wasn't an explanation because this showed the public that I had never stumbled or fallen during my whole time in the competition. There was no reason for the show to eliminate me. I received a standing ovation after my last performance task and I had been a perfect contender the whole time.

Looking me in the eyes on my way out, Winona Waters mouthed the same words Marcella had just moments earlier. *I'm sorry!*

It was so frustrating that I didn't know what they were sorry for exactly, that I really had no idea why or who had made this decision. As we exited through the competition room doors, the ever-present cameras waited for us, preyed on us, hoping to catch us crying or get footage of our angry faces because we had not made it through. Several of the other kids who had also been eliminated were begging, crying and screaming. I didn't do that. I just walked. I kept walking, past the cameras and past the crew. My head was held high and I stopped as a video producer ushered a camera person towards me.

"NOA, are you disappointed in the judge's decision?" she questioned, a microphone shoved invasively in my direction.

"It wasn't the judge's decision, and I'm pretty certain you know that."

I knew they couldn't use that on television. It would out the show as being rigged. She stared at me for a cold moment before asking another question.

"Do you feel as though this is it for NOA?"

"NOA was working fine before this show and will be fine after this show."

At this stage, I was holding back tears (there was no way I was going to let them see me cry, not if my life depended on it, and it felt a little as though it did). I put my head down and made my way as fast as I could to my dressing room. I could see from the corner of my eyes that Senses had been eliminated as well. This didn't make any sense to me, especially after the night prior and the connections that I saw they had. I had assumed that they were completely safe.

Almost running now, I turned towards the elevator doors and collided with somebody in black. I looked up, but couldn't see as my eyes were filled with yet-to-be-cried tears. The figure reached up and wiped my tears away. Through the blur, I could see it was Marcella.

"I'm sorry they did this to you, NOA," she said. "It was because you figured out too much... they know that you know what's going on."

Chapter Twelve

Experiments and Calamities

Experimenting and trying out new things often leads to realisations. For example, I remember going on a date once with a girl who convinced me that a deep fried Mars bar was better than eating regular chocolate. I've always hated chocolate, which is why I was annoyed when, on my seventh birthday, I bit into the cake my father had bought me that said happy eighth birthday, only to find it was made of chocolate. And again, when my date and I ordered the deep fried Mars bar, I remembered, in that moment, how disgusting chocolate actually was. Experimenting can be a good thing. It can reinforce what you already know or open you up to new experiences, but it can also leave you with conclusions that you thought could never exist.

*

This was probably one of the lowest points in my life. I came home the night I was evicted from the show's hotel, to a room that was clean and spotless. My mother had cleaned my room and had bought me new bed sheets. It was a very strange thing to find. I usually never allow anyone into my room. I was really grateful for my mother's thoughtful act because I needed a clean pillow to cry on. The clean room showed me how much she cared and the new sheets were a bit of luxury that I needed in that moment. It is small things like this that remind me how much I do love my mother, regardless of what we've been through.

I fell asleep that night with only one person in my mind: my ex-girlfriend.

It is funny how, in moments like these, all you want to feel is loved by a special somebody. Caitlyn and I had always been an explosive duo. She had cheated on me numerous times and we constantly fought over the smallest of things. We had been on and off for about five years at this point, and it was at this moment that I wished she knew how I was feeling. I didn't need her toxicity and drama in my life; I was striving to achieve, to reach the top, and I had decided to cut her out of my life. Still though, I lay there wishing she would tell me that everything was going to be okay.

*

Shortly after I finished had school, Caitlyn and I were invited to a friend's birthday party. We had recently got back together after I had caught her making out with another guy, who was one of our friends, in the school bathroom during our graduation. We were supposed to go to the school formal together, but each of us ended up going alone.

At this friend's birthday party, I had two experiences that confirmed my own evaluation of my sexuality. Caitlyn and I were both drunk and decided it would be a good idea to hook up and get back together. I remember, in a quite passionately violent way, pushing her up on the laundry washing machine and kissing her unlike I have ever kissed anyone before. To this day, she still admits it was the best kiss she's ever had, and I would say the same. There was something about the urgency and chemistry of that kiss that set our passions alight.

It was everything you would expect it to be from two teenagers who had grown up in love. I had known Caitlyn from many years prior to us getting into a relationship. We had noticed each other when we were about eight or nine. I had finished Kitty Kat Sundays and joined in a combined school choir. All the schools in Western Sydney, came together every year to put on a magnificent show of dancing and singing, where each school could showcase their students' talents. Being from different schools, Caitlyn and I admired each other from afar. She would watch me from her school queue, stand and sing alone. This was one of the many perks of being a chosen soloist: alone with a backup choir. There were only ten solo positions each year and for every year I had participated in the production, I had been chosen by the city talent teachers to sing alone. Each year, I had noticed Caitlyn in her school's dance troupe. She had brown doe-like eyes, danced like a ballerina and was the prettiest girl I had ever seen.

It was many years later when Caitlyn walked into my high school that we struck up a friendship and were inseparable. We fell hard in love and this love destroyed us. An English teacher at university once described this kind of love as the best love one can experience. She called it: tragic love. A type of love where you care for somebody else so much that you end up sabotaging yourself and your relationship in your attempts to ensure that you will remain together forever. Oftentimes, this leads to the ultimate destruction of this love and the love dies, hence the tragedy.

It has been written about throughout history; Anthony and Cleopatra, Romeo and Juliet, Whitney and Bobby, Sonny and Cher.

I recall the birthday girl's mum coming into her laundry, outraged as she saw us on the brink of a sexual encounter. But this did not stop us. We moved on and continued in the bathroom, keeping at it, like any teenagers would, with hormones raging. She was not a virgin, but I was. I remember her begging me to have sex with her. To me, losing my virginity would have been like giving her a prize. She was proud of already having had sex and was proud to have had other relationships in-between ours. Call me old-fashioned, but I wanted to wait until marriage. Giving in would mean that she won or had something over me. It just wasn't me. Believe me, a part of me wanted to have sex with her as much as she wanted to have sex with me; to solidify our love and make it concrete and forever. I guess this is where star-crossed tragedy comes into play. I couldn't bring myself to do it drunk though. I wanted her to want me while she had a clear head, not while she was intoxicated... like she had been with the other guys she had slept with. I was worth more than a quick, drunken hook up and I thought she was too.

I pulled away from her and went upstairs to find my close friends, Victoria and Drita, and let them know that Caitlyn and I were back together. Someone overheard me and accused me of being a liar because they had just witnessed Caitlyn downstairs making out with a boy named Gregory. I called her a moron and went downstairs to find Caitlyn to squash the rumours and drama. But, returning to the party, I witnessed Caitlyn and Gregory lip-locking right in front of me. Without thinking, I grabbed a glass bottle of alcohol and launched it in their direction. I was so angry! I hated her and I couldn't care less what happened to him.

Crying hysterically, I ran upstairs to the embrace of Drita and Victoria who had seen Caitlyn do this to me too many times before. To this day, I thank them for listening to all my Caitlyn crap.

As expected, Caitlyn had fled the party and Gregory was left with a cut on his brow. I had done everything trying to please this girl, trying to be what she wanted me to be. She had called me fat, so I lost weight and ended up getting quite sick for a few months during school. Everybody thought I was stressed from studying, because I was quite academically bright at school, but the truth of the matter was that I was starving myself to please Caitlyn. I had even changed the way that I dressed because she had called me 'too feminine' to want to be with. I couldn't understand how someone that I loved so much would do this to me, just like I couldn't understand how something like Star Power, that I had dreamed of being a part of since I was a kid, could destroy me.

I went downstairs to apologise to the birthday girl's mother for my behavior and then decided to leave. It was on my way out that Gregory pulled me into the corner of the living room where nobody was and told me that he wanted to speak to me. Reluctantly, I followed him to apologise to him because, at the end of the day, he didn't know we had just hooked up. It had been Caitlyn's choice to betray me, not his. It was at this point where things got really strange and I began to question the whole gay thing again. There had been numerous times in my childhood, as I have discussed earlier, that bullies during school would call me a 'fag' or a 'homo' because of the way I behaved and dressed. The more times you hear the same thing, the more you begin to question the legitimacy of what is being said. I knew who I was as a person, but hearing the same thing over and over as a child can confuse you. Gregory leaned in close to me and whispered a sexual innuendo. I can't remember what he said, but I was taken aback and certain things have become blurred in my memory. I knew I wasn't gay, but I remember thinking that if I did anything with him, I would be getting back at Caitlyn. I would get revenge and, for once, I would be the winner of a most dramatic plot twist. We began making out. I was drunk and didn't really care at this point. I didn't really think about what I was really doing until he touched me inappropriately.

I realised what was happening and I pushed him away and told him to 'Fuck off.' The irony was that he was actually one of my classmates who had taunted me during lunch at school for being gay. His behavior that night couldn't be gayer, but I guess this taught me that I wasn't the only one who had ever questioned their sexuality. I ran out of the house and vomited. This wasn't who I was. I wasn't gay, I wasn't a cheater and most of all I wasn't a vengeful person. In a strange way, I am glad that these events unfolded as they did. I remember feeling disgusted for not remaining true to myself and realising I could never be sexually attracted to a guy ever again. I wasn't disgusted by Gregory; I didn't find gay guys repulsive—if I see a good looking human—male or female—I will let them know, but hooking up with guys just wasn't me, it wasn't who I am.

*

A few weeks had passed since my time in the competition and I was in a downward spiral of depression. I didn't eat, I didn't want to go out and I didn't sing. I had been calling Caitlyn regularly since the night that I had thought about her and she had been answering my calls. Yes, Caitlyn had re-entered my life, bringing with her all the unnecessary drama that I had forgotten and that I didn't need. At this point, we were reaching the eighth year of our on and off relationship and I just couldn't handle it anymore. I already felt pathetic with the events that had transpired on the show and I sure as hell didn't want to feel like a loser when I was with my girlfriend. She was still cheating and wouldn't go anywhere with me in public because, to her, I was an embarrassment. She said I looked gay and was a failure at what I had tried to accomplish.

Once again, I found myself in a place of confusion. Even my own girlfriend called me gay. I was sick of people's assumptions and was getting tired of everybody trying to box me into being something I was not, just because of the way that I dressed and carried myself. I had already fallen into doubt from all this before and here I was going there again because of everyone else's opinions. I had feared being exploited on national television about this very thing, and now there was all the Caitlyn stuff to deal with. Our contracts for the show had stated that the producers were allowed to manipulate footage in any way they wanted to and, at this point, I was convinced they were going to catch my worst moments and air them so that I came across as gay.

To prove everyone wrong, I decided to download a dating app and go and have sex with some random girl to 'get it over with'. That, I decided, would shut the world up. I knew I was straight and it annoyed me that people just sat there judging me all the time. If a child is feminine and they're gay, they are either bullied for it or told 'it's okay, you're born this way and you're beautiful'. If you're straight and fit into society's pre-conceived gender descriptions, then you don't have a problem, you're accepted for who you are. But for me, I was straight and also feminine, so I didn't fit the 'norm'. Where did this leave me? Where did this leave all the other children and teenagers out there who were straight, but who acted differently, who were a little too feminine to be your typical male, or too butch to be your typical female? Where was our support? Most children become convinced, like I was almost convinced, that they are gay because people keep calling them that. If you hear the same thing every day, it's hard not to associate yourself with the word. To this day, I hear the word gay and turn around thinking that someone is taunting me, which is why I have such great love and support for the gay community; I know what it's like to be bullied because of your sexual orientation and the way you look and behave. I believe there are children out there who don't know who they are yet and are forced to live a certain way to meet expectations. It is okay to be whatever you want to be and behave however you like. It is important to know that you don't have to conform and become gay because you're a feminine male, or a lesbian because you're a masculine female. You're a certain way because that is who you are, that is what makes you unique. By the same token, if you are gay, lesbian, bisexual or transgender, you shouldn't have to bow down to fear and hide in the closet. Have courage. Just be yourself.

After chatting to a random woman on this dating app for a few days, I decided it was time to do the deed. She invited me to her home to 'experiment' and I made my way in my shabby old car to her house. My car was twenty years old and cost two hundred dollars to buy. Even though my father was a mechanic, he decided to duct tape the brakes, give it a clean and re-dip the tyres in rubber to make it look new, rather than fix it up so I would have a safe and reliable car. In actuality, it had broken down on me three times already and my father didn't really care. You would think as a mechanic, he would help me buy a car that actually worked, but this was not the case.

Anyway, I drove to this woman's home, thinking I was ready for it. I knocked on the door and she led me inside. She was in her late thirties and was basically what the world calls a cougar—or so I thought. My little sexual experiment ended up a disaster. As she led me into her home, I couldn't stop staring at her ass. She was quite fit for an older woman and she had this very seductive husky voice. I finally looked around her home and I noticed photographs in of a family: herself, a husband and two children. She wasn't a cougar, she was a MILF. It was at this point that I started to feel guilty. I was not going to allow this woman to defile me while cheating on her husband. In one sense, I was proud that a hot thirty-something year old wanted to have sex with me, but this was not who I was. I realised that I didn't need to do this in order to prove anything to anyone.

She walked towards her bedroom door and instructed me to meet her in five minutes. That I did not do. I grabbed my keys and bolted for the front door. I ran to my car, turned the engine on, hoping it wasn't going to die on me, and I cried all the way home.

What the actual fuck are you doing, NOA? I thought to myself. *You don't need to prove anything to anyone. You know who you are. Enough is enough. Get up and stop being a little bitch. You've sat and cried for weeks. When the right girl comes along, you will know. Get rid of Caitlyn and start doing something with your life.*

*

Music is what kept me going at this point. I began experimenting with new sounds and looking back on songs that I had already written with Ted. I didn't want to give Ted the satisfaction of seeing me release one of our pre-recorded tracks, so I tried to incorporate my melodies and lyrics to other music.

I had come up with the idea to release a single the moment the show aired and I was finally on television. I still wasn't sure if they would air me at all because some contestants were just on the show to fill up a room or to make it seem as though the whole show was a genuine competition. However, I knew that if they did air me in a positive light, I would need to release a song quick smart so that I could remain relevant and in the public eye. In hindsight, I was lucky that I didn't go further into the competition. Had I made it to the next round, according to my contract, I would have been unable to release any music for twelve months.

In a way, being booted off at that point was a blessing in disguise. So many friends I had made were stuck with these contracts after the show finished airing and were unable to release any music. They risked being forgotten by the public. Their contracts had these 'no release' clauses so that no one was competing with the winner after the show had finished. After all, it would not reflect well on the show if an eliminated contestant was able to make a bigger impact than the actual winner. The show added these clauses into the contracts to halt the rise of the unsuccessful contestants. Lucky for me, I didn't have any such contract.

I was convinced that with a good song, I could exploit the platform the show would give me and make an impact. But as you may know from reading so far, I never do things in small portions. I wasn't just going to release a song, I was going to film my first ever music video and release it with the song. Working with Ted and his label had allowed me to learn the process. So many broken promises and plans allowed me to know what not to do and how to organise things the way that I wanted.

I reworked a song titled 'Villain' and experimented using different instruments from a range of cultures. I wanted this song to be something familiar, but also something people had never heard before. In a way, this kind of defined who I was. Researching my favourite singers and how they made it to the top, I found that they were all strange in some way, like I was. They didn't quite fit in, but this afforded them the luxury to experiment with their music and to send their messages out to their listeners. I wanted this for my own song.

The days passed and I sat in my room reworking chords and melodies on my laptop music program. I knew what I wanted this song to sound like, but I didn't have the skills to produce it on my own. I decided to email a demo to a few music producers and production companies. The responses came in, and I was told that my song was too different and too experimental for them to take any risks.

Just as I had given up hope, a producer named Sammy called.

Chapter Thirteen

Anaphylaxis

Determination is a valuable asset. Personally, I believe that determination is a great skill and a powerful ability to have. Talent is one thing, but the more determined you are, the more success you will achieve. I also believe in that saying, "Don't put all your eggs in one basket." I have always said that it's important to put your eggs into several different baskets, rather than just the one. This way, at least one of those eggs will hatch and the probability of having an egg hatch in each of your baskets becomes possible. In saying this, you must be determined to equally tend to all of the baskets and care for each of the eggs. This is determination. Making sure that, at all costs, you have an avenue of some sort to achieve your dreams. You should let nothing stop your ambition and drive. The moment you lack this determination is the moment you lose hope. With determination, no matter what you go through, your head will be held up high, even when you think you cannot cope.

*

After contacting numerous producers and songwriters to help me on my journey, I discovered Sammy, a producer who had worked with a variety of Australian artists and had mastered a few famous electronic albums, like The Ministry Of Sound CDs. I was hesitant to hire him at first as he worked at Studios A-G, who were known for being very prestigious and very expensive. I just didn't have the type of money it would take to work with Studios A-G, but I did have a few thousand dollars put aside from my childhood career that I was happy to use to fund this new venture.

If I wanted to make sure I made an impact on the show, I had to have a single released the day that I was 'kicked off'. This would cause a stir and make people listen to and hopefully buy the track. Even better, they would wonder why I left the show (which was never clearly explained on television) and would want to know what I was up to. When these viewers visited my social media pages, I wanted them to see that I was still kicking and that nothing was going to stop me. This was just the beginning.

I eliminated a few other producers by default and I decided that Sammy was somebody I wanted to work with. I would have to find a way to foot Studios A-G's bill. I knew it was overpriced, but Lady Gaga, Michael Jackson and Madonna had all recorded there at some point on their tours in Australia. I needed to include my name here, whether others liked it or not.

At this point I had lost my driver's licence so my mother had to drive me about an hour away from where we lived to drop me off in the heart of Sydney city to begin recording. The time slot I had been given by Studios A-G was 8pm-4am. It was the cheapest slot they had available and my mother supported me by agreeing to pick me up early in the wee hours of that morning after we had finished and before her shift at the take-away shop.

Before we left home, I made sure I was dressed to impress. First impressions are everything in this business. Rocking my bleach-blonde man-bun, a thick, gold chain and bright yellow tracksuit, I stepped into the car, my white winged sneakers flapping behind me. My relationship with my mother wasn't the best during this time in my life as she was struggling with the last few years of marriage to my father. It was always a difficult task to be around her. She yelled the whole way there and I had to work hard to keep my composure and stop myself from crying before we arrived.

Two massive, intimidating, black, iron gates faced me when we arrived at the address and I got out of the car. To the right of these gates was a speaker. I pressed a button next to the intercom for them to let me in.

Sorry, you are visiting the studios after hours. Please use the side gate.

I had this thought at the time that I was already not good enough to enter the front of the bloody building, but this made me feel more determined than ever. Entering from a side gate behind a bush, I made my way around what seemed like a huge campus-style block of land. It was some time before I found where I was supposed to be.

Waiting outside the building was Sammy. To be quite honest, he didn't look like a musician and had two dogs with him running around the front of the building. Now I'm not one to judge by appearance, but he certainly did not look the part of an established producer.

"Hi," he said, sticking his hand out to shake mine, "I'm Sammy, I'm very interested in and happy to work with you!"

As we introduced ourselves to each other, we began discussing what I wanted and how long it would take to record. Entering the studio building, we were met with construction workers and removalists who were doing some type of refurbishment on the place. Sammy looked at me in embarrassment and apologised on behalf of the company for this intrusion. By the time the movers and builders were finished it was 2am and we had only a couple of hours remaining of my booking time.

"Look NOA, I'm really sorry about this." Sammy apologised, "In all honesty, that's just not how a song is made. Your track needs more than eight hours to be perfected. You need days, sometimes weeks to perfect a song. Some songs take months and years until they're ready. You haven't booked in enough time for us to make sure you leave here with a great and finished product. For that, you're looking at a minimum of about five sessions or forty hours."

I held back my tears.

*

Years before, the announcement of the newly-formed school choir had irritated me. You had to be over seven years old to try out and I was short just three months. I had begged the head of the choir to let me audition so I could join, but I was flatly refused because I was deemed not 'mature' enough. I'm not sure how the maturity level of a child changes that much in the space of three months, let alone the year from six to seven, but nonetheless I was denied entry into the little choir they had created.

As you may well know by now, this was not an answer I was going to simply accept. I ended up joining the choir and getting scouted during our performance by Mr Myers, the director of Kitty Kat Sundays. It was because of this experience that my dreams started becoming a reality and I was allowed so many opportunities. The way I got into the choir, however, will leave most of you in wonderment.

The day had arrived, after a week of auditioning grades 2 to 6 students, that the school choir participants would be revealed. As my primary principal read out the list of pupils who had been accepted into the school's performing arts choir, I just couldn't hold back my frustration. Being six, emotions were something I had not yet learnt to control. Rather than to holding in my anger, I decided it would be a better idea to 'crash' the principal's speech and so I walked up in front of the school. One of the teachers tried to coax me back into my seat on the grass where all of the students were sitting cross-legged. It was an outdoor assembly and every child had their hat on and polo shirt buttoned up. Our school colours were yellow and maroon; two lovely colours that together look very ugly. As the teacher's hand reached out to stop me from getting up, I shrugged her off and, with my very stubby six-year-old legs, marched my way up to where the principal was standing. Unfortunately, I do not recall the name of my primary principal as I was only at this specific school for three years before moving to another district school that was, luckily, under the same performing arts community schools branch.

I reached the principal's one step podium and I grabbed his pants, jerking them up and down to get him to pay me some attention. Leaning downwards, he asked me if I was okay and what I was doing out of my seat. I responded by telling him that I had something to say to the school. He looked at me as if it was his own personal risk allowing me to speak, but hesitantly gave the microphone over to me anyway. This was something that now, as a fellow educator, I truly still admire. He didn't know what I was going to say, but I like to think he saw something in my eyes that made it seem important, and he let me address the school of over three hundred students and teachers.

To be quite honest with you, I don't know why I started singing the national anthem, perhaps it was because the school was very Western orientated and most of the faculty and students were from an Australian background, but regardless of my reasons, I belted out Australia's home song. I laugh when I think that I must have had marketing on my brain even back then. Somehow I knew that, for this particular audience, Advance Australia Fair would be a winning anthem. I finished the song and the whole school applauded me for my natural ability and courage. The principal thanked me and publically suggested that I join the choir.

Nothing is impossible if you're determined to be brave enough and to have courage.

*

Fearing that the song and recording would be potentially cancelled, I made my way home with my mother, sulking all the way. I went straight into my room, hoping for some type of miracle. It wasn't my fault that nothing was set up at those studios. I didn't know how much time it actually took to perfect a song. From what I knew and what I was used to with Ted, it only took a couple of hours. Now I realise that it only took a couple of hours because Ted did not actually master and mix my music properly.

I woke up the next morning with a missed call from Sammy. I pictured his grimacing face and his rectangular-shaped glasses and contemplated not calling him back at all. I understood that the situation had not been his fault, but I was still annoyed that, as somebody who worked for the studios, he hadn't done much to rectify the situation with the builders. Reluctantly, I returned his call and we started speaking. He explained that he was genuinely sorry for the mishap and wanted to make me a promise. I asked him what the promise was and he told me that he would personally promise to finish the song in all its completion due to the lack of organisation from the studios. He felt he owed me this.

From his explanation the night prior, I had calculated the cost of the labour needed to complete the whole song. Mixing and mastering costs came to over a thousand dollars alone, let alone producing and creating the track. Altogether, I figured I eventually saved myself about six thousand dollars.

Sammy invited me to the studios again the following week to continue to record. My experience the second time around was nothing but extraordinary. It was a complete contrast to my first encounter there. I walked into a large studio space, bigger than my previously assigned room. Sammy had made sure that I got the very best out of his promise, and for that I am still grateful. I believe that if you carry yourself courteously and behave respectfully toward people, you invite them others to be respectful and generous to you in return.

At the studios this time, we had interns who were there to treat us with beverages and food. They were available to us on call at any time for basically anything we needed. I really felt like a professional musician, but I still never let anything go to my head. I was there to work and I was there to make my song perfect.

Most recording sessions require the artist to sing the vocals and watch as the producer then mixes them. This is sometimes a tedious task as hours can go by with you just sitting and watching as the producer mixes and creates the music around your vocals. I never lazed around, I was here to make the most of this time. I watched to see what Sammy was doing so I could potentially mimic his skills and be able to produce one day myself. I had done this with Ted, but, as we have figured out, his skills were not the best. Although Ted had a natural flair and an ear for music, he was unable to master and mix songs at all. However, Ted's producing was fantastic, which is why I began to focus on the way Sammy mixed the music and moulded vocals and instruments together on the same track. Believe me when I say that this is a difficult thing to do. Despite this challenging task, there was something about working with Sammy that made song writing feel effortless again. We just understood each other. We simply connected with the music. I had explained to him that I wanted the track to take stylistic genre turns. With every change of verse or chorus I wanted the listeners to hear a different influence, yet I also wanted it to connect with itself and be a complete body of work. Most people would have called me crazy. You can't mix a genre halfway through or add in an instrument that doesn't belong into a random place. But Sammy understood me. Did he look at me like I was crazy? Absolutely, but as we began to build a friendship, he really understood my point of view as an artist and began enjoying creating new music that hadn't been made public yet. It was a different sound and had a different essence to everything else that was out at that time.

*

After a few sessions in the studio, I was asked by Sammy to come in one last time to finish of my final vocals. I went prepared and warmed up, having downed my little vocal elixir: garlic, lemon, honey, ginger and tea, before I arrived. I got there at about nine in the evening and was greeted by the regular intern who told me that Sammy had ordered dinner for us.

While we waited for dinner to arrive, Sammy got me to go straight into the vocal booth to start recording. Luckily I was warmed up because the final part of recording included the bridge, which was the highest part of the song and required a high-pitched head voice. It wasn't out of my range, but there were high notes in the song. After singing very high for a while, getting tired is inevitable. I didn't care though. I wasn't going to show that I was tired, I was going to give one hundred percent.

The intern arrived with dinner and we took a break to eat because Sammy had been working on another album from the morning. He asked me if I enjoyed sushi and I had told him that I didn't mind it. I was unaware at this point what the difference between sushi and sashimi was. I enjoyed cooked chicken sushi or a chicken schnitzel sushi, but I was completely in the dark about raw fish or anything that was uncooked. Coming from an ethnic family, uncooked food wasn't a delicacy and it wasn't something we ate. With my family, everything was overcooked: steaks, chicken, lamb on the spit. Raw fish was not my friend, which isn't surprising since I have never even enjoyed eating cooked fish. If there had been a poll between poultry and seafood, I would have voted for poultry in a heartbeat.

Placing the uncooked, slimy, raw fish outside of its container, Sammy smiled and said, 'Bon Appetit.' I watched in horror as the fish slimed down his throat. That was definitely not 'Bon Appetit', it was more like 'Bon Absolutely Not!' But I didn't want to offend anyone, so I grabbed the plastic chopsticks that came with the container and shoved a piece down my mouth. Using chopsticks correctly has always been important to me; I feel cultured when I eat with them and will always use chopsticks when eating traditional Asian cuisine.

"This is actually quite nice!" I exclaimed to Sammy, who was smiling with his thumbs up in excitement.

From the moment I met Sammy, he was always pushing me to do and try new things, this was another extension of his personality. What he was unaware of was that I didn't think this food was nice at all; I actually couldn't swallow it because it smelt like the sea and was just a gross texture. Grabbing some water, I tried to get rid of the aftertaste. Then I was back in the booth to continue to sing the parts we needed to record. While I was singing, I noticed that I felt a furry feeling in the back of my throat like it was beginning to close up.

Oh God! You have to be kidding me.

I began to sweat... profusely. I thought I was going to die.

Sammy noticed something was wrong, but as I turned to him my face grew its own shaded mask and I gave him a look as if there was nothing wrong at all.

"All good, Sammy, play the verse back!" I ordered him.

He had no idea what was going on. I didn't care about anything at this point. All I wanted was for the song to be finished. The show would commence airing in a few weeks and I needed the song to be finished so that if I was aired, the public had something to go to and watch and enjoy.

I messaged my mother to bring an EPIPEN when she came to pick me up. I had recorded two hours' worth of vocals with a constricted vocal cord and while having a near death experience. My mother arrived after we had finished and punctured my leg with the EPIPEN to stop the allergic reaction.

The thing is, in this business, you can never afford to give up, anaphylaxis or not, you just have to keep going.

Chapter Fourteen

Videos, Vultures and Villains

After the song had been completed. Sammy and I made an agreement to keep working on music together. He almost became my manager, of sorts, just like Ted had been. The difference was that Sammy allowed me to expand my creative horizons and helped me to grow by myself rather than trying to control things. Sammy was always in support of me trying new things and doing things on my own, as well as stepping in and helping me when I needed him.

The airdate of the show was fast approaching and I needed to make sure that, by the time I was kicked off the show, I had a song and video out there to promote. I knew that people would be wondering why I had not gotten through to the final rounds of the competition. I never gave a bad performance and, therefore, there would be no reason for me not to be there. I had to show all of my fans and supporters that I was still active and was still going to pursue my dream. After all, so many young kids looked up to artists on these shows, just like I had growing up. I needed to show them that it was possible to keep going, and that elimination from the show did not mean your dreams were over. Most of the artists that get kicked off these shows are never heard of again. This is often because they are offered a deal to shut up and sit on the sidelines so they don't get in the way of the main artists, who are promoted and marketed to the masses by the main record labels. Another reason the competitors are never heard of again is because of the post-traumatic stress disorder we all experienced and the horrific reminder that we had been rejected on national television, in front of the whole country. Some people, unfortunately, just don't recover from that.

*

Stepping into a strange looking studio apartment-style block, I pressed a button that read 'Sunwide Studios'. These studios were connected to many radio stations and owned artist access to radio play and most magazines in Australia. A deal with these people would be the same deal that I could have gotten if I had won the show. I was excited to have been invited and waited for the person behind the intercom to let me through. The invitation I received to meet with this label was quite a surprise as I'd had ties to the label from when I was on Kitty Kat Sundays and I had not heard from them in a very long time. Struggling with doing everything on my own, I was intrigued to find out what they could be offering me, considering I had been part of their company some time ago. Obviously there would be new management and new staff, but I assumed there would be some loyalty on their behalf which would allow them to offer something that could help me.

Walking into the building, I felt my anxiety and excitement rising. *What could they want from me?* I stepped into the lobby and a lady at reception immediately asked me my name and sat me in a waiting room. While I didn't know it then, this room would be the only room I was going to see at this place. I waited for about twenty minutes, looking at all the platinum record awards that adorned their feature wall. There was a cow skin rug at my feet and huge nest-shaped leather chairs that I felt were too fancy to sit on. The place had changed a lot. Above me was a large chandelier; this had obviously become a very rich establishment since its start-up days. I sat on the couch, comfortably waiting.

A man much shorter than myself and wearing a suit and tie entered the room and apologised for making me wait. I was wearing a navy blue and black jumpsuit-style pantsuit, with a medium length blonde wig and large gold hoop earrings. I looked like I could just have easily walked onto a fashion runway straight after our meeting finished because I was dressed the part and looked like a true artist.

"I'm sorry NOA, my boss is actually out having a root canal today and totally forgot that he had this meeting with you. If you don't mind, I'm a partner at this record label and would love to interview you myself, if that's okay?"

Fantastic. I had not come here to meet with the understudy of one of Australia's largest record labels. I came to meet with the boss.

Almost right away, I knew that there was no point in this conversation going further, but I sat and amused him regardless. Even if your gut warns you about a potential outcome in a situation, I advise you to always stay until the very end. You don't know what you will discover. Anything can happen.

"So what we, at Sunwide Studios, would like to offer you is what we call a 'Development Deal'. This means that, for two years, you will be given access to our recording premises to create music and be offered to work with hundreds of our top producers."

The word 'development' was the word that instantly turned me off the whole conversation. I had been in this situation before with Ted and a few other small labels when I was growing up. 'Development' means that, in the label's opinion, you need to still develop yourself and come up with a sound and an image. I already had an image and sound, why would I need developing? I already had access to a studio and recording services. What benefit would I have gotten from this 'development' deal?

"I'm sorry Dennis, but what exactly does this development deal contain in regards to releases?" I asked. "Will there be a release of this music at some point or will I have wasted two years for nothing and have no access or control over any of my songs?"

He paused as he realised that I wasn't the idiot he was hoping for. They had probably done this to hundreds of young singers to shelve them or steal their intellectual property. Shelving would mean signing only to never release anything, for it to be 'put it on a shelf' to get dusty. These deals sign artists only to quieten them and restrict them from releasing their own music, essentially so that up-and-coming artists don't affect their 'top stars' or their sales. It would be terrible if Beyoncé released a song and in the same week a newcomer knocked her off the charts. Development deals are given to up and coming stars, not to help them, but to hide them away so that there is no threat to a studio's headliners. Labels like this need to keep up their good reputation; sometimes, if they find another unsigned artist who is threatening the reputation of their headliners, the studios will try to silence the threat and development deals are a perfect way to, not only silence the artist, but also steal from the artist. Once these kids write songs on development deals, the label can choose to reproduce or rewrite any of that material. After all, the label is paying for the facilities and the producers who are making the beats. Therefore, the artist ends up owning nothing and not being able to keep any of their musical rights other than their lyrics. In this case, all the label has to do is rewrite the words, give it to Katy Perry, or some other more established artist, and there's your song on somebody else's album. What aggravated me was that so many kids would have fallen for this while following their big dreams to become a pop star. It was a tragic, manipulative trick that spelt disaster for up-and-coming artists.

"Well, NOA, this deal is only to develop you and help you discover who you are. What happens after that will happen after we see growth and development from this contract. We cannot guarantee anything, however, there is a very high chance you could be a star after this. Would you like the paperwork?"

"No, thank you, Dennis, it sounds to me like the 'development deal' you speak of is only being offered to artists who you would like to 'develop' songs from in order to steal their material and plagiarise it for other parties. You know most up-and-coming artists can't afford to sue you for stealing their work, so you manipulate them into giving you free song writing, with clauses that eliminate the rights to their own royalties and share of the work. I will be releasing my own music, thank you very much. You have a nice day."

In situations like this, you need to remain firm, strong and resolute in your determination. Not many people turn down a recording agreement. In my eyes, it would just make any music mogul who knew of me angrier that I wasn't shutting up... and that's exactly what I wanted them to know. I wasn't going anywhere and neither was my music.

*

The ring around to find a director for the music video was ultimately a struggle. So many videographers were asking for thousands upon thousands of dollars and I knew that that amount of money was something I couldn't afford and that I could find someone to do it cheaper. It was quite by accident that I found Terrence, just like I had found Sammy. I was Googling videographers when I stumbled across an online reel of amazing photographs and pictures. *I wonder if he does videos?*

I called Terrance and he revealed that he had filmed for a couple of nature documentaries in Australia, but had never filmed or directed a music video; he was, however, eager to try one and add that to his own list of accomplishments. Hesitating, I asked him the cost and he suggested five thousand dollars.

Using this much money meant almost wiping out half of the savings that I had collected over my years of working at a DVD store and tutoring English to young kids. Looking at my finances, I concluded that I wasn't allowed to touch my Kitty Kat Sundays' money because I wanted to appear responsible to my mother. In all adults' eyes, my musical aspirations were just a dream of hope rather than an occupation. Becoming a famous singer or actor is not often considered a proper job due to the huge risks that the job brings with it. There's no set wage or guaranteed success rate. Some days you get paid, other days you're the one paying to get ahead. I had to do this with my own money and my own funds, especially if it was going to be the first production under my own self-created label.

I didn't say yes to Terrence at first; you should never say yes on the spot to anyone, it's important to keep your options open before making a final decision. I kept looking around and tried to find someone who could do the job at a cheaper rate. The cost for something like this was between twenty to fifty thousand dollars. Terrance was the only option I had at that time who would ensure we would finish the video in two months. It needed to come out the moment that the show aired. With negotiation, Terrence dropped the price to four thousand and got another three individuals on board to help with production: a cameraman, director of photography and a lighting technician.

While I was doing all this planning, I was also dealing with a slight legal battle with Ted. He had musically and legally registered the first version of 'Villain' under his name and my name, conjointly. This meant that I wasn't going to be able to release it on my own without permission from Ted, with half of all proceeds going to him. This version of the song was completely different and new. Luckily enough, Ted's threat of keeping the song was empty and he signed the rights over to me after a week or so. He had also given me an electronic keyboard the day he signed the rights over. I refused to take anything from him, but he insisted I take it to practise my song writing skills. The only reason I ended up taking it was because I knew he had a very large hard drive of all the songs we had recorded over three years that I was never going to get back. I also felt, in a strange way, like, he felt guilty about screwing me over and needed to mentally have his own peace of mind about what he had done. That I will never know.

After meeting with Terrence one last time, I decided that going through with this project would be the best thing for me. He had a team of people who really wanted to participate in this video and the passion they had for making something exciting is what fuelled my decision. It wasn't about money anymore; it was about the craft.

*

Two weeks passed and I found myself on the set of my first music video. It wasn't like everything I had ever dreamed of, but it was a dream come true nonetheless. My cousins, Cyril and Ellen, had come with me. Ellen was in charge of driving us and Cyril was there to be my personal assistant for the day. We arrived at our location, which was a huge, white, photoshoot studio, at about six in the morning. What was clever about this studio was that it had an infinity wall, which meant all of the walls and the floor of the room were white and had no corners, creating the effect that there was only one wall that went on and on forever. Terrence and the crew began rigging up the lights and necessary video materials while I finished getting my hair and make-up done. I had booked the premises for eight hours, so that was all the time we had. I had five costume changes and the song was four minutes long. It was a feat that needed to be done and, of course, we pulled it off.

What people don't know is that making a music video is a very long and tiring process. Just like song recording, you have to film and record the same thing about a hundred times until you get a perfect shot, or until you have enough material to work with in order to manipulate a perfect shot through the editing process. Additionally, you need to film the same thing from different angles, which means even more time on set. The lights are boiling hot and the dancing and singing soon becomes a very tiring process. I remember forgetting to eat. I became so consumed in punching this project out that I really, unfortunately, don't remember a whole lot of the day. I was too focused on making the video perfect and I never actually stopped to enjoy myself and or to be proud of what I had achieved. I am the type who usually gets caught up in the moment, but in a strange way I'm glad the video turned out so fantastic; there is no way it would have looked as good as it did had I not been vigilant and persistent. I do recall one fun shot that we filmed where I stood on a 360-degree moving disc while the camera followed me around. This created a 3D effect. What viewers of the video don't know, was that there was actually a crew member who had to spin my feet from the bottom in order to create that spinning effect! I guess I remember that part because I thought it was kind of an innovative shot that I had not seen before. Another hilarious event that took place was when I walked too far backwards into the infinity wall assuming I had extra room to dance in. The walls and floors were so white and so perfectly clean, it was impossible to find where the room actually stopped. It just looked like an endless white sea.

The video was all about fashion and style. I wanted a fashion look-book video. When the show aired, I wanted this video to be something viewers and the public could watch and really understand who I was and what image I was trying to portray. I wanted them to understand that I was different and I was coming onto the scene as a new, but polished performer who knew exactly what he wanted and who he wanted to become.

It was also quite exciting because I landed a few promotional deals from this video. I had clothing companies that I was already a huge fan of send me an array of tracksuits, I had a designer send me shoes and I was lucky enough to also meet and work with amazing stylists and hairdressers on this quest to finish my video.

After what felt like a knick of time, but was actually six hours of shooting, we got through five outfits and I was more than happy with the end result. It was one of the best feelings in the world. I actually accomplished what I had always wanted to do and, with sheer determination, I had done it on my own. None of the other contestants would have shot or recorded a hit song or a music video to go with it. It was a kind of, 'here I am' moment. I definitely was not camera shy and the outfits and performances I gave to the camera embodied everything I wanted NOA to be: fashion forward, tough, stylish, polished, talented and creative.

I questioned the competition again: Who really had the most talent? Had they put any of these kids in a recording studio? Put them on set? Were any of them filming a music video? Could any of them fund and organise a whole production by themselves and have it finished and ready within two months?

Chapter Fifteen

Blacklisted

Anxiety had crept upon me in the lead up to the show airing on television. The villain music video was in post-production and was almost completed, but there was always the possibility that the show's producers would cut my whole presence from the show. It was not unusual for them to just wipe people out as if they had never been there. It had happened before to a few other friends of mine; their hard work on the show remained unacknowledged, the stress they had felt was all for nothing.

I was on my guard during the whole period of time between filming the show and it airing months later. I had shot my video and recorded my song, I had landed promotional deals with fashion labels and had also contracted deals with local magazines and newspapers so they could promote and publicise my audition and position on the show. The agreement with most of these publications was that, once the show aired, an interview would be printed in the publication about my new single release and about my experience on the show. Nobody set this up for me, I did this all on my own and was proud to say that for somebody who was determined to succeed, I was trying my damn hardest.

The show aired a few weeks later and while most of the audition episodes had already been shown on television, my audition was still yet to be shown. Friends and family who knew I had auditioned and had passed through a fair few amount of rounds on the show, were constantly asking when the airdate would be. I couldn't reply because I simply didn't know. I did not know what the show was going to do with their footage of me, I didn't know how their editing would make me look, and I had no idea if any of their footage of me would even be aired.

Fortunately for me, the last audition episode aired was my episode. I made it after all, but they set me up to look like a diva with an over the top personality; I mean, I guess they probably got all this when they fed me lines during filming, but their careful editing seemed to exaggerate everything I had said and done. As a television viewer, I would have assumed that the person, who was presented as they had presented me, was a complete idiot. The green screen video-box interviews were pretentious and producers made out my story to be one of self-involvement and self-adoration. In my interviews, I had discussed that I wanted to be a singer because I wanted to be an example to all of the kids out there who had been knocked down in life as I had been. I wanted to show other hopefuls that anything was possible and that music could be a great outlet to those who wanted to rise above their current reality. There have been plenty of songs during my life that have helped me cope and helped me through hard times. I wanted to reiterate that music can change your mood and that the benefits of listening to and playing music are mostly positive. However, the only thing they decided to air was me with all this attitude and sass, talking about my clothes and my likeness to other American artists. Don't get me wrong, I do admire these artists, but I do not like being compared to them because the aim of my musicianship is to create something new from the influences of these artists. You can't be new if somebody keeps comparing or pushing you into another person's box.

*

The episode aired to an amazing reaction from the Australian public. I was expecting online hate and bullying for being different, but that's not what I received. People actually loved my rendition of the song I sang and they loved my rapping. The Australian audience had fallen in love with my charisma and voice, and I had fallen in love with them. Overnight, my audition was uploaded by the show onto their official online video channel. It received over one million views in twenty-four hours: it had gone viral! At this point in time I was astounded. One million people had seen me sing, over one hundred thousand people had liked the video on social media while thousands of people had shared it. I remember looking to the sky and thanking God for hearing my prayers. It seemed that Australia liked the sass after all! I mean, part of my personality is sassy and brash, but that's not all that I am. I was just glad that the public at least liked what they had been shown.

A problem arose, however, two days later when the video the show had uploaded was removed. In hindsight, I understand why the show pulled down this particular video, but at the time when it happened I became a very angry person. I didn't know why they had chosen to do this to me and why they would seemingly purposely hinder my career and hurt me personally by doing this. The reason, I later found out, was because I was getting a bigger hype than the contestants who were still on the show. Announcing my exit from the show would have caused a public outrage, which is why they never aired me getting kicked off. I somehow just vanished after a few episodes. As the next couple of rounds aired on television, I was simply phased out; none of my other performances were shown! Had the producers shown me receiving a standing ovation, the public would have questioned the judges and their legitimacy. How could they say I was amazing and then kick me off? That wouldn't have made sense, so they just chose to delete me from the rest of the show altogether. The producers of the show were obviously not expecting that I was going to receive that much support and, unfortunately for me, I had to be removed. I became a threat to the show and a threat to the winner.

I had also come to the conclusion that most of the media in Australia was interconnected. The radio stations and magazines that I had landed interviews with to discuss my new single called to tell me that my slots had been replaced. They had replaced my interviews with ones that included contestants who were still on the show. Why? Because a major Australian media company owned the show. They owned the channel the show aired on, along with half of the major national newspapers and magazines. This company, and their rival company, controlled almost every part of Australia's national media: the rival company owned the other main channel on television at the time and the other national press papers. The Australian media was basically split into two monopolies. I was unable to contact or be a part of the rival company because I had signed a contract stating that I was unable to 'hop' companies. The company that ran the show had, in a sense, blacklisted me from being on any forms of public national media. The more I was shown in magazines or on television, the more people would like me. The producers wanted to stop this from happening because they wanted the planned winner of the show to get the most media exposure and make the most money for them. While I'm sure the rival company would have loved to take me in, I was legally bound by my Star Power contract. I couldn't appear in any public press release with any company other than Star Power's head corporation and, as I've explained, the corporation needed me hidden.

I was uninvited to shopping mall performances that the producers organised every year in local suburbs to promote the show. I was uninvited from appearing in their magazines. I was uninvited from attending the show's promotional shoot. This is what it meant to be eliminated from the show.

As you may know by now, I am not a quitter, I do not silence easily and I do not walk away from my dreams. I had re-uploaded my audition onto the Internet and even got myself in copyright trouble with the artist who originally sang the song I chose to audition with. My version was an updated cover and the show had not cleared the copyright for it. Usually the music producers approve contestants' songs so these problems don't occur. But this time, the show had not cleared the copyright or asked permission from the original artist's label to rearrange his song. That meant that my audition would never be allowed to be released or uploaded onto the Internet again without me risking being sued by the original artist's management. I had personally been warned by the artist's management to stop uploading the video. While I understood the original artist's perspective, the situation felt very unfair to me because most of the other contestants had been copyright approved and their videos continued to go viral. Once again, my progress was hindered.

At this point there was nothing much I could really do, other than promote my new single, Villain, and hope that it would somehow resonate with listeners. Radio airplay was a no-go because the company also owned half of the radio stations in Australia; I legally was not allowed rotation on the other radio stations because of the clause about company rivalry in the contract I had signed initially. Television was out of the picture, so in the end I did the only thing I could do and I turned to social media to try to promote the song as much as I could. Villain's release marked a historic event to me in my life. The song was trending nationally on social media on the day of its release and really made an impact with fans of the show. They loved the song and loved the video that I had spent so much time and money on. It felt like such a relief. It was the only thread that was holding my career together. Without having the idea of releasing the song during this period, I would have had nothing to push my name out there. I would have been forgotten, like so many other artists who had come before me.

*

At the time, and to this day, I was grateful to my friends, family and fans who helped my song reach the top forty on the national electronic charts. My hard work was finally being recognised, but the burn of the company which produced the show and what I had uncovered while on the show was still burdening me every day. It was at this point that I reconvened my difficult relationship with Caitlyn, again. My best friend Drita's sister, Joanna, described my relationship with Caitlyn as tumultuous and one that was beginning to look like a dysfunctional safety net. When you're in trouble or in need, you can end up falling or crawling into a ball of protection; at this time Caitlyn was my protection. She gave me that companionship that is intrinsic to any human being. Did it make me feel better at that moment? Yes. The repercussions, however, were disastrous.

Not once did I ever stray from my career though. I was hustling to organise a signing tour under my own label (managing myself) across Australia. During this tour, I was able to meet with many of my true fans who had known about my career from years before the show. It was an incredible experience to travel my country and meet these remarkable people, who also had their own dreams and ambitious and who were all supporting my journey.

It was also ironic that my first live performance after the show, was opening for Serenity Hayes, the winner of the previous season of Star Power. I was performing on the same stage as the winner of the last year's show. The other competitors were still trying to battle for a record deal and for public approval. I had already been offered a place to perform next to a winner. In my eyes, that made me a winner in my own right. I already had a top forty song, I was performing with a former winner and I had released my own music video. That is what everybody on the show was striving for… and I did it on my own without any record label backing me up. I was also fortunate enough to open for an Adelaide Fashion gig that allowed me to really feel like a touring artist, travelling alone and performing my own material—material I loved, to an audience who may not have known who I was.

Throughout this period I became a very diligently occupied person. I threw all my emotions into my career and that is what drove me to whatever success I achieved during that time. Unfortunately, I was unaware of the personal affect all this effort was beginning to have on me. Shortly after the airing of my episode and the promotion of my first song around the country, I started to have nightmares about the way I had been eliminated and about being blacklisted from the entire music media in Australia. I would wake up in the middle of the night screaming or in tears as I relived my time on the show with these people hacking my livelihood. The producers became demons trying to steal my voice and media personalities became grim reapers who kept hewing at my limbs and replacing me with other contestants. Ursula from The Little Mermaid even made some appearances in my nightmares as she tried to capture my voice and place it in her shell—just as she had done with Ariel's. I could only describe the ordeal as post-traumatic stress. I wasn't eating or sleeping properly and although I was positively focusing on my career and music, I didn't understand the detrimental effects that it was all having on me.

Sadly, I also learnt that success can push people away from you. I lost many friends who assumed I was putting myself selfishly before them by travelling and by trying to get ahead in my own life and career. Other friends saw my successes and jealousy became a catalyst for them walking out of my life. Fame and the music industry are things that most people don't really comprehend. Natalie, who also experienced something similar with her girl group, Senses, was the only person I felt I could really relate to at this point. None of my other friends, or even my family, could really wrap their heads around what I was going through. Natalie was able to relate closely because we shared a collective memory of the same events. Through our discussions, we unravelled more and more of the show's secrets: plotted winners, plans and intentions. The show was a nasty business that revolved around quick money and revenue. They didn't want to risk a contestant going global because that would mean a split in revenue with overseas companies. They needed to choose someone who was going to be famous enough in Australia, but not too famous they could potentially sign a deal outside of our country's borders.

Looking at Australian musical history at that time, not one contestant from these television programs had made it big overseas. Only a handful of ex-contestants or winners were able to make a small influential imprint (over ten years later) once they broke away from the show's stigma. Risks were not something the show was going to take. It didn't guarantee them ratings or money for their turnover each year.

What burned me the most was that people liked what I was doing and I knew I had the talent and passion to make a name for myself internationally. I was lucky that Sammy, my new producer, saw something different in my spirit and was happy and willing to work with me on it. Without any hesitation he offered to produce my next music singles and material and became somebody I could trust.

To me, Villain was the most perfect song written to release as my first single. It was a definite message to all the media outlets and producers of the company and television channel: I'm never going to quit and I will be the bad guy if I have to be. Sometimes to get to the top you have to be harsh. This doesn't mean you're a horrible person. My whole life I've been intrigued by the villains in fairy tales and their side of traditional stories that have been told. On television, you only see one side of the story. You only see what the producers plan for you to see as presented through cutting and editing. My songs and this book are my story. I may have been a villain or perhaps I am seen as a sore loser for 'back chatting' or 'slandering', but I, like so many contestants before me, was hurt. To me, it wasn't about who won the show or the fact that somebody could have beaten me. It was about the lack of fairness of the whole program. I felt like the show set people up for failure. I mean, don't fly contestants out from another state just to embarrass them on national television. Don't feed people lines simply for the amusement of television audiences. Don't edit my performance so that it looks like nobody was interested when I know the crowd gave me a standing ovation. This is and was my own personal recollection of these events. Sure, we all have different perceptions, and what I feel is the truth, another might dispute, but just because I have decided to air out my opinion doesn't mean I am the bad guy. But at the end of the day, if the shoe fits, I am proud to wear it.

*

After the signing tour was over, my relationship with Caitlyn only got worse. Now, after almost nine years of an on again-off again relationship, she decided to take her abuse to a whole new level and physically hit me at a friend's social gathering that we were attending as a couple. I decided to call it quits for good. I couldn't stand to be in a physically violent relationship, I wasn't going to become my mother and I wasn't prepared to relive the violence of my childhood, but my heart was absolutely broken. I felt rejected by colleagues and peers in the industry who I had grown up with, all because of one company that seemingly ruled the world, or at least that's how it felt at times. And, through physical violence, I felt rejected by the one girl I had loved for so long. My safety net was well and truly gone and I was left alone with nothing but this feeling of injustice. I could find no resolution or closure from the experience. It was unfair. Had the show explained why or how the elimination process worked, then perhaps the anger would have more easily subsidised. However, nothing was ever explained, not in the beginning, not at any stage throughout the filming of the show and not upon elimination. Everyone cut me off.

I can't explain the strangeness of the situation and the emotional state that I was in during this period. I don't think I have ever worked so ambitiously or diligently in my life as I did at this time, but I was also so broken and so angry. I had to find ways to do everything on my own. Creating my own business, selling my music on accredited streams, royalty recognition, nationally registering and approving my material, music videos, sales projections, music, recording material, writing lyrics and melodies... the list goes on. I felt like I had been stabbed by so many people, but without these wounds, I would have never become the hero that I became.

The nightmares still haven't stopped, but I have managed to work them into my life as lessons rather than as the traumatising experiences they once were. I believe that my relationship with Caitlyn was there because she allowed me to feel human heartache and heartbreak, which led to the creation of so many great songs throughout the writing process and demo stages of my career.

The show was also one of the most significant occurrences to ever have happened in my life. It allowed me to recognise that evil is meticulous by nature, not serendipitous. People do bad things purposely in order to achieve their own desires. My goal became: being a singer who told stories through their music while standing up for those people who didn't have a strong enough voice for themselves. Nobody should be treated unjustly and nobody should experience this type of ruthless pain. It felt like the Hunger Games, only nobody died in real life. It was psychological warfare, but there was no way I was going to be quiet. If the show was only going to air a half a story and if they were going to blacklist me from all media outlets, then I was going to air the other half of the story through my music and create my own outlet through which to reach people, and writing this book became one avenue to do so. My next song was going to be a small win. It felt like my duty to be a voice for people who were considered not 'normal', who were 'unusual', who took risks or were seen as 'risky'. This became my calling.

Sorry that I didn't fit into your cloned, moulded standard of a pop star. Sorry I was too much of a risk to bother with. Sorry I had ambition. Sorry I was smarter than the normal contestant who just believed everything you painted. Sorry I was actually liked by the public and you had to get rid of me because I would have ruined your plans.

Actually... I'm NOT SORRY at all!

Chapter Sixteen

Dressed to Impress

Fashion is a means of self-expression and making impressions. The clothes on our back are a way of revealing personality traits and characteristics that we perpetually hold. I'll add that this form of representation, I believe, has nothing to do with gender. Personally, I don't see fashion as masculine or feminine; I see fashion as a means of self-pronouncement, which should be interchangeable between genders. While trends in fashion range from the mundane to the fantastic, and various styles come in and out of favour, my fashion sense doesn't always affiliate to what's in vogue. If I like it, I'll buy it, it's as simple as that. I've always been an advocate for the blending of the expensive with the cheap. Not everything has to be designer! While I would love to be decked out in custom-made Atelier pieces that was just not possible while I was growing up. I was able to save enough money to buy one fairly expensive piece, like a pricy jacket, but then I would pair it with a two-dollar tee and ten dollar jeans. It's not what you wear that really matters, it's how you wear it.

Clothing can also become a uniform, a mask or piece of armour to keep others at bay. Your sense of style and dress can reveal to another person the way in which you choose to present yourself and this can be perceived by others in stereotypical ways: someone in board shorts and a Quiksilver tee can be stereotyped as a surfer even though they might never have surfed in their life.

Clothes are a way for me to express my emotions and my primary disposition. However, what most individuals need to realise is that this sense of identity and choice of clothing changes over time, sometimes it even changes daily. I don't always want to look like a perfect Ken Barbie doll. Some days I grow out the beard, put on some glasses and a cap and become that hot, next door neighbour who the girls are always staring at. On other days, I want to shave the beard completely, put on a cake face of make-up like a Kardashian and walk out leaving the girls next door wishing they looked as pretty as me. It's all about choice, the way I feel on any particular day and the way I wish to be perceived at different times and in different situations of my life.

*

My buzz from the first promotional single was dying down and I needed to ensure that I still remained present in the underground and social media scenes. Another signing tour around three major cities of Australia was a great way to accomplish this. I remember meeting my fans as they recalled their stories and hardships with me. I was able to create a connection with some of them that I will never forget. It meant the most to me that at the time; I was still a 'nobody', yet they saw something special in me and wanted to show their support.

The signing tour was predominantly used to promote the first single and now that a couple of months had passed, I needed to once again stop the media from pacifying my climb to the top. I was still having terrible nightmares about the inconclusiveness of the show and its decision to eliminate me after my best performance that they never aired. This unexpressed anger and frustration caused a reaction in me to keep fighting and to prove to everyone that I was meant to be a forerunner in the competition. It also caused a stir in me to let everyone know that it wasn't simply about the competition anymore and it wasn't just about my music either. It was about showing these companies and these media platforms that I was a capable artist in my own right, with the possibility of making it on my own without their help.

The next studio session, with Sammy, sparked the idea of my second promotional single, Regal Disaster. I wanted the song to be a mesh of Arabian Nights meets electronic pop. This was the first song I had ever written for which I had a predetermined view about what the outcome would be. Even before I had started to write it, visually I knew exactly what I wanted.

It was imperative that I cause another commotion with my next promotional music release in order to keep media interest in my music at a high. The show was in the middle of its air run of that year, and at this time, people's speculations about my exit from the show were beginning to die down. It's true when they say: you only get fifteen minutes of fame. The public gets over you quickly. Statistics show that only about one percent of your fan audience truly has an emotional connection to you after seeing you. That percentage changes the more and more they see you, as they become familiar with you and come to see you as part of their friendship group or family, and thus you become a household name. It was my aim to show the Australian public that I could produce yet another successful video clip, along with a song that was unique and different.

This time, I would bring in animals. No one in Australia was as ambitious as I was at the time. Nobody without a label was going to release a video with animals. It was too much of an effort and most of these labels don't care about the message of the video. They wanted a quick, green-screen film clip, as cheap as they could get so that they didn't waste money and could ensure a quick release date. My intention, however, was to surprise my audience and the music media by going above and beyond, providing them with a video that had a message and was metaphoric: something you could watch over and over, gaining new things from each viewing. It was also my way of showing the music executives of the show that I was going to do it bigger and better than they would for their winner's first video clip.
*

I've loved fashion ever since I was a kid. Watching The Spice Girls on television and seeing them in magazines, I used to rummage through my mother's cupboard full of platform wedge shoes from the 80s and 90s and strut around the house pretending I was Scary Spice. It had always been my dream to be able to wear clothes that none of my other classmates would ever wear or could ever get their hands on.

During my time at school, students were allowed to come to school, once a term, in 'mufti' clothes—non-uniform outfits. I was always the best dressed. One thing that I always found difficult as a male though, was the ability to stay on trend and wear fashionable clothes. Men's fashion, though some might not agree with me here, doesn't really change much, season to season, in terms of structural pattern work. It's always a jeans-and-shirt or a suit-and-tie outfit. Sure, patterns, length and fit might change, but the idea of a man having more than a couple of options to wear has always been quite limiting. Although I always maintained my sophistication, I became a walking, blurred blend masculinity and femininity: which is, I guess, how NOA came to be. Most fashion trends are created for females because it's a given fact that females consume and count for more than 75% of the apparel industry.

It was during this time that I struggled with wanting to remain fashionable, but not wanting to present myself as too female, traditional male or homosexual. I wanted to blur the lines. As I've mentioned before, I don't have a problem with being any of these identities, but these stereotyped identities are not who I am.

I had to find a happy medium that suited me. Androgyny is a perfect word that comes to mind. I became hard, but soft at the same time; delicate like a flower, but harsh as a thorn.

Society and the people around me allowed for this creation of NOA to exist. I had felt constrained by fashion, it wasn't that I was scared of putting on eyeliner or wearing a ponytail, it was the fact that I craved the social aspects of fitting in, especially during high school. I think everyone feels that way during school, they just want to belong. Dressing and behaving this way in school meant having a hot alert right above your forehead. I wanted to stand out, but I didn't want to be so different as to be ostracised.

I use my box analogy to describe my creation of NOA as the simultaneous blend of masculine and feminine. Imagine it this way...

It's almost as if I was boxed in by what everybody wanted me to be and I struggled to push out of that box and maintain my individuality; however, in the process of sitting in that box, I decided that if I had to be here, the box at least should be decorated from the inside out. I was still inside the box, but my box was prettier than everyone else's. I guess that's a great way to explain it. I created something to protect myself from the sharks and bullies of the world who would say I was too different if I expressed myself as I knew I could. Yet I maintained my individuality and my different image, so that people could speculate, but never really know.

If you think about this idea, it's quite clever and almost inheritably animalistic. Most people can't take the pressure of hiding their individuality and either break through the box to reveal their true form or cave in and stay in the box, never breaking free and revealing who they truly are. In my situation, I've created a way for the box to be manipulated. I am free to remain in my box, but I also have a door to step through whenever I want. I'm comfortable in my own skin. Sometimes that skin sheds and sometimes it regrows. But at the end of the day, it's still my skin. It took me years to really understand this concept. I don't believe we are what we wear; I believe that what we choose to wear is how we present ourselves and who we appear to be to others. This choice is ours, and ours alone, to portray to other people. I love being loved by people. It's a complexity I've had since I was a child, which is why I love being on stage. And on that note, it excites me when I see men and women who are attracted to my self-created beauty. On a psychological level this may seem odd, but I've socially and visually constructed myself to appeal to all people: all races and all genders. I'm girly, but still masculine; I'm white, but slightly Eurasian; I'm all kinds of attitude, yet I am timid at the same time. You may want to ignore me, but you can't... and before you know it, you will look at me. I'm designed to be beautiful, almost like a vampire. I've created NOA to be the most socially and visually constructed version of likeability that exists.

Perhaps it was my obsession with Barbie dolls. I used to love playing with my sister's toys as a kid. It became my job to design new clothes for the dolls because my parents were struggling financially and we couldn't afford to keep spending money on Barbie outfits. My grandmother had been a seamstress during the 70s and had taught me how to use a needle and thread. I recall one afternoon during the school holidays when I ripped down her yellow floral curtain to make a dress for my sister, Christine's Barbie dolls. My father had come to pick us up later that evening and I remember frantically running to hide the leftover material and the doll that was in my hand. My mother had warned me that when my father was around I had to hide the dolls—I was not to let my father see me playing with dolls. I know that she was trying to protect me, but to this day I don't understand why a child should need protection from its own father. A father should surely encourage their child's play and individually rather than behaving in any aggressive or sexist manner.

I thought I had a few more seconds before my father barged through the door, but there he was, happy to see his kids who he hadn't seen in weeks after neglecting, us as usual. And I guess this was a happy occasion for him because we were now his part-time children. It's like holding a baby: it's cute for an hour and then the responsibilities kick in, or the baby cries, so you give it back to the mother. That's how it seemed to be for my sister and I and our father. The moment he saw the doll in my hand was the moment I ran. I ran as fast as I could to get upstairs and to the safety of my grandmother, but I wasn't fast enough. Before I knew it, I was slammed into the wedge behind the room's door and squashed by the hulking weight of my father.

"What have I told you about that shit?" he yelled, the tone of his voice threatening destruction.

I remember that harrowing moment as I struggled to breathe as he began squashing me between the wall and the door. The doll had dropped and I remember thinking that as long as he didn't touch the doll I would be happy, because the dress I had created for the doll was really perfectly made. It's funny how, as a kid, you don't realise that abuse is actually abuse. This kind of thing was normal for me and my household, and so it wasn't until much later that I actually came to the realisation that this was considered abusive behaviour.

This experience, along with many other similar outbursts from my father over the years, allowed me to witness the strong effect that image has on people. You can paint on a happy face and go to school, and others will think you have a 'normal' family life. You can be a lesbian and dress like a man, but it doesn't mean you are male, it simply means that you are dressing and representing yourself in the way you wish. Certain clothing has a certain reflective meaning. You create meaning with what you wrap your body in. This has nothing to do with gender identity or who you are on the inside. It's what you choose to show on the outside to others that counts.

*

I had organised to film my next music clip in central Australia, right between the border of South Australia and the Northern Territory. My lovely dancers, who had performed with me for the Adelaide fashion event on one of my signing tours, decided to come on board and join the project. I was fortunate enough to have met some lovely crew members, directors, make-up artists and hair stylists who all held a belief in me that I would do some good. They joined the project and a few months later we embarked to the middle of Australia to shoot my music video, complete with camels, in the desert.

The shoot in the desert was unlike anything I had ever experienced. The dancers and I had to be awake at four in the morning to get the ball rolling, while hair and make-up arrived shortly thereafter. We had to be completely ready by six to head to our destination three hours away. The camels greeted us as we arrived and to be quite honest the experience was miraculous. Three large golden creatures appeared and sat hovering over our van as we turned onto the dirt road. It was quite extraordinary. Their regal presence seemed to make everything calmer. And this was quite fitting, after all, the song was called Regal!

The temperature outside that day was fifty degrees Celsius. To this day I am so thankful to every team member, dancer, hair and make-up artist who withstood the weather with me. The air-con in the van wasn't working properly and the heat was just unbearable. I was actually perched up on a camel's back for over five hours in the blistering heat wearing a velvet, Jeremy Scott, matador jacket that weighed over three kilograms. I remember the sun burning through my leather shoes along with the sandy desert burning my eyes every time wind caught the area. It was something I had to endure. It was a test of my character and a test of my patience. There was probably no other person I knew who was this determined to strive for what they wanted to achieve. I remember almost fainting at one point and one of the dancers passing me up water while I still remained on the camel.

The sight would have been absolutely ridiculous with me holding an umbrella over my head to block out the sun whilst also still riding the camel. If a by passer-by had seen me, I would have looked like an ethnic, modern, Arabian-style Mary Poppins in the middle of the desert, but of course there were no passers-by as we were in a stinking hot, isolated desert in the middle of Australia. Looking back now, I see the humour in this completely. At the time though, it was just hard work.

The director on this shoot worked completely opposite to the way the director of the Villain video had worked. He used a technique whereby he played back all the footage he had shot and then reviewed and fixed it all before reshooting. When I say review, I mean he actually sat there and watched the video play back in slow motion while I struggled to stay alive on that camel! This process literally takes three times longer because you actually have to wait for the director to review what they've just shot. I was getting frustrated because I wanted them to just hurry up and shoot what they could. The director's father was also a film maker and he was the one keeping everyone calm that whole day. There was a sort of Zen about him that turned the stinging heat of the sun into energy for us. We filmed until dusk and eventually got home the next day at about four in the morning. We had been awake and in the heat for over twenty-four hours.

There was no way in hell that any other contestant from the show was going to have a film clip like I had, let alone have the endurance to participate in or accomplish a project like mine. I had high-end fashion designers who had collaborated with me and were appearing at the New York Fashion Week the following year. I had custom-made clothing and clothing that was privately sponsored to me. We had dancing, singing, rapping... and camels: the whole gig. There was nothing less than amazing about this video. I had worked part-time for many months to save the thousands of dollars that was going into this production and was so grateful that so many people had come on board for free to help me pursue my dreams. I will never, ever forget that aspect of the project and will be forever thankful.

The camels were gorgeous and I was lucky enough to have ridden on Camille the Camel who was a first place, camel racing champion. While she did decide that my drop down Versace earring was food and almost rip my earlobe off, I found her to be absolutely gorgeous and fascinating. I've always been an animal lover and I adored the fact that I was able (with all the animal laws) to shoot a music video correctly, by the book, myself. No shady business, just hard work.

To my surprise (not really surprise, mainly annoyance), the music company that ran the show had also decided to release the winner's film clip in the same fortnight as my second release. It was funny because the winner was just starting up their engine, whereas this felt like my second coming. I was already a step ahead. The videos came out and mine was received well by fans and critics. While it did not garner as much exposure as my first release, it did manage to chart on the music charts even higher than my former single. So despite a drop in social viewing numbers, business numbers increased, which was a great thing. The winner of the show had their music video pulled down by the show's record company for being too cheap and looking like it had been filmed on a budget. The irony was that the replacement video they filmed included an exotic animal. *Wow...* I thought to myself. *Coincidence?* I think not. I was reminded of the saying, *imitation is the greatest form of flattery*.

Chapter Seventeen

The Hurdle up the Mountain

There are plenty of occasions in life where it feels like the mountain is getting too hard to climb. It is my personal belief that it is in these situations where an individual's integrity can be measured. That is not to say that those who fail to keep climbing lack integrity, but this idea of climbing a mountain adds to my notion of choices. We all have a choice: to stop or keep climbing, to follow the hardest route possible or to decide on a more positive path up the mountain. Perhaps that path allows for a rest on the way up. I'm the type of person to critique those who fall away due to fear of failure. But remember, no matter how hard the climb, there is always a way to the summit. Your inner strength formulates your course of action and sets your resolve to continue your ascent. There's always a way to move forward, you just have to find it.

*

My mountain, like most other mountains, has not been smooth or easy to climb. There were several occasions where I did want to just quit and tumble back to the base of the peak. But something inside me wouldn't allow that to happen. I recall a point where the abuse from my father struck at a whole new level. My parents' relationship at this point was acrimonious and my father's quest to abuse us was at an all-time high. He had run over my mother and had kicked her out of the house, leaving my sister and myself to fend for ourselves. It was around the Christmas period as I recall attending a friend's birthday event. At the event, my 'friends' at the time decided it would be a great idea to spike my drink with all sorts of alcohol. To this day I am unaware of the contents of that drink. According to a close friend who had been there, I appeared 'dead to the world.' There were tough guys taking pictures of me passed out and I'm not sure how, but I ended up waking up the next morning with a cat lying next to me in my friend's guest room, fully clothed, but in totally different clothes than I had arrived in the evening before. According to someone there, these people were making fun of my situation, snapping pictures and poking fun at the obvious joke of the night: me.

During the course of this intoxication, I realised my life was not okay. I was, according to the people present at the party, screaming for help, telling everybody that my father had physically assaulted me and my family. I was airing out all the dirty laundry that my family had held so closely hidden. I was also crying (which is something I rarely do as I have learnt to always try to keep it together) and explaining to everybody how I had been taken advantage of by Star Power and how it wasn't fair that I was still stuck in the hole that I called my home.

I've always known that the premeditated act of spiking someone's drink is atrocious; nobody should ever be tricked into consuming something they are unaware of by having their drink tampered with. Despite this, I came to see this incident as a double-edged blessing in disguise. Rather than dwell on the negative experience and become a victim of it, I decided to look for whatever insights I could find from the outcome of the night. The whole experience made me realise that I had been choking. I hadn't dealt with anything properly. Not my parents' split, not the abuse we all suffered at the hands of my father and not the trauma I experienced from the show. The nightmares were still present and my ability to comprehend long explanations or stories had become limited because my mind was constantly drifting to things like getting back on the show or getting back at the show. It was almost like I was consumed by negativity. I was falling down the mountain; I had forgotten to anchor my ropes to the rock face, to tie myself to a harness.

I'm not really one to ask for help or seek any mental health advice. I've been raised in a very orthodox environment where you deal with your own issues and any type of mental illness is frowned upon. This conditioning still colours my views today and I must admit that I still have difficulty understanding mental health issues, yet I promise you, there are days where I feel like I'm going insane, as well as days where I am just at a really harrowing low. Psychological help was out of the picture for me, as this 'tough' mentality and 'no doctor' policy had been ground into me as a child, so I was once again left to my own devices to try to figure out the problem. My family, although dysfunctional from the beginning, was now actually falling apart physically before my eyes. I had no girlfriend and had lost many friends due to them not understanding my musical commitments. I was quite alone and I knew had to figure it out, smart and quick. I realised that the more I tried to fight the show, the more I was going to lose and the more stressed

I would be by staying in this negative space. I mean, what could little old me do to change an industry that had been running in Australia for fifty odd years. I couldn't change something that was already set in stone. What I could do though was to place a stone beside it, and to start to build my own mountain next to it. Yes, I may have started out as a pebble, but if you can't beat them, build next to them. Show them that you have immense drive, passion and commitment, show them that you are stone with big ambitions to become your own mountain.

*

My aim in this industry is to create a platform where others are able to showcase their talent and get help where I had received none. I decided to give up-and-coming directors, producers and photographers new opportunities by choosing to work with them, instead of turning to the already established individuals who I knew had money and a career already. It was through this process that I found happiness again.

On my signing tour, I had met two lovely fans who had gone above and beyond my expectations to get my name out there in their little hometown outside Melbourne. I swear that, because of them, I'm somewhat famous in that town. They promoted my music in shopping centres by handing out flyers and also created their own social media fan following service. I had to meet them! I made an effort to buy them some gifts and pay them a visit while I was in Melbourne.

It was through them that I met a young, aspiring videographer by the name of Jaquez. He may have been young, but he was a really great filmmaker. After stalking his Facebook profile, I invited him to join the girls and me for lunch where I asked if he would shoot my next music video. Of course, without hesitation, he said yes. I explained that if it wasn't great it wouldn't be released. I was giving him a chance and I had faith that he would not let me down, but I also had to warn him that this was a business and it needed to look amazing.

The third in a trilogy of songs, titled Tornado, was released a few weeks later. I had come to the point where writing music ended up being the most therapeutic thing for me to do. It was a way to explore my pain, to make sense of the confusion, to express myself and to heal past trauma. Writing about my experiences through the use of metaphors also allowed me to write great music and, with the help of Sammy, I felt that these songs could be hugely successful. My third song also charted well and all three of them became a triad that I deem to be one of the most personal pieces of work that I've ever put out to fans. Jaquez also shot half of the music video and worked together with me to create something magical. I found it quite ironic that he got me to climb up a rocky wall near the edge of a beach in Melbourne for the video shoot. It was a witty analogy of my life and I realised that while I was climbing these rocks I was coming face to face with the idea that through these accomplishments and feats I had started to climb my mountain again.

*

Contracts with these shows get ridiculously complicated the further into the competition you get. During this period of working extremely hard to put out more and more music on my own, I met up with a few friends (and competitors from the show) that I had made along the mountainous path the show had provided. There were some contestants who were aware that the show possessed the ability to create predetermined outcomes, while others argued (because they were gaining success and had remained on the show for longer) that the way the show functioned was actually fair. I'm the type of person who, although I had gained a reasonable amount of credit for being on the show, had always acknowledged my peers who never got in, like Belle who I met at my very first audition. I was not better than her because I had gotten through and she hadn't. She worked hard to make a go of singing and she had her own career as a back-up singer; she held her own accomplishments. It surprised me that there were a few contestants who, it seemed to me, felt as if I was 'beneath them' because they had achieved a greater level of success on the show. What they failed to understand was the aftermath that the show's contracts would have on them.

The tables turned when the show finished and the contestants who had made it to further rounds than I had were bound by stricter contracts and weren't able to release or promote themselves in any form for a whole year. Whereas I was releasing my singles and videos while these performers had to put a pause on all releases in case they gained a considerable amount of success, to become a threat to the winner's popularity and record sales. It was at this point that I witnessed the whole thing as a kind of blessing in disguise. Had I not been removed from the show at the point that I had, I would not have had the opportunity to release my singles and accomplish what I had achieved in such a short period of time. My passion and drive were what kept me going, kept me wanting to prove that I was just as good as anybody else on that show.

There were a few amazing competitors who I did meet and who I still speak to occasionally. Some of them felt the harsh reality of selling out for fame; one of them actually agreed to join a pop group on the show and ended up getting dropped and disbanded by the second month out from the airing date. Some others I kept a regular affiliation with, but after a while most of these friendships kind of fizzled out. We were friends on the surface because we had shared the same extraordinary experience. Other than that, we didn't have much in common and we didn't really know each other.

Through these catch-ups and coffees though, I discovered more and more about the way the show actually worked. We all discussed the show when we were together because that was the only true commonality we had to talk about. Some had told me that during the live performance rounds (which I did not get into), contestants were kicked off the show because of their refusal to wear specific outfits and costumes. I wasn't shocked by this information, surprised that the show's Machiavellian strategies were still coming into play well after I had gone. There was a story told to me by an ex-contestant that a group of African-American girls were kicked out because the show couldn't understand how to deal with African-American hair; that the cost for weaves and wigs was an irrelevant cost. Now I'm not sure how true that comment was, but for it to have been repeated I believe there was probably some veracity to it. I found things like this to be disturbing and almost disgraceful coming from a company who was supposed to cherish individuality and promote multiculturalism. The winner, whose film clip mimicked mine, was also selected to win that year so that Australia could show its Asian neighbours how supportive they were of Asian arts and talents. There had been a political rift between Asian and Australia and one theory was that this particular winner had won in order to settle the perturbed concerns Asia had with Australia, to promote something oriental and unique. Again, I'm not sure to what extent this is true, however, I do believe that a company that has a massive press and multi-media outlet like theirs, would love to influence politics and other international broadcasting.

It was strange that the usual age categories every year on Star Power had been under 25 boys, under 15 girls, groups and over 25s, but the particular year I was present, the winner was in the over 25 category at just 24 years old... Had they changed a whole category just so that she could win? Had they brought her back after kicking her off because of politics? She had been kicked off like I had, but she was brought back without an explanation, into a category that she wasn't even registered in or eligible for. Perhaps I would have been too expensive for them to keep on the show, what with my needed expensive outfits and hair and make-up.

*

While the other ex-competitors were having a forced rest on their own mountains, I was lucky enough to be able to keep climbing without any contracts holding me down. Unfortunately, Sammy decided to relocate to the USA and I was left without a producer for quite some time. It was during this period without him that I decided I could no longer wait for him to produce for me. I needed to get more material out there and keep it coming constantly. I have always said that it doesn't matter who sees what you do in the present. There will be a point in the future where people look at your past and see your accomplishments and how you've gotten to where you are. I wanted to show people that I did remain consistent with releases and never stopped practising my craft or learning new things.

Momentarily losing Sammy to his overseas venture, I was forced to start producing on my own and creating my own music... completely alone. It was almost like first learning to rap. Nobody could help me so I had to help myself. I had to make my own beats and my own piano chords to my own lyrics. At first I was quite scared and thought that everything I was writing sounded like rubbish. I guess in that sense I was, and still am, my own worst critic; everything had to be perfect all of the time. Because of this fear that my own music would be almost detritus compared to my other songs, I decided it would be a good opportunity to release some remixes while I mastered the new skills necessary to produce my own music. I had always written the main shell of my own songs, but I had never mastered anything completely in terms of musical production. I knew basic piano chords and I had my lyrics and melodies. Every time I released something, I felt like it needed to be better or more unique than the track before it, like I needed to be constantly improving on my previous work. It was because of this that I put my next single away until the perfect time came.

*

My first mixtape, Samurai, hit number one on the urban, free download charts in Australia. It was an amazing feat, but also a shame that the musical material wasn't mine. Due to musical copyright laws, you can't sell music that isn't yours without permission. To get permission, you need to either pay royalties or an upfront amount to use the samples you wish to place in your records. I didn't have this type of money and I decided it would be a good way to give something free to all my fans out there as a thank you for their support.

I have always admired the idea of a mixtape. Most of the kids in my neighbourhood didn't have money for new CDs, so we used to buy one single CD each and then burn all of the tracks together onto a blank CD or blank tape to listen to. In all parts of the globe, this practice is where the idea of a mixtape originated. In the US, mixtapes became an opportunity for young Hip-Hop artists in Brooklyn, Chicago and New York to get their music heard by burning their tracks onto CDs. They would slip these into music stores so people would hear them and thus would get their name around their suburbs. I loved this cultural reference and so I decided that it was a very street-style, underdog kind of thing for me to do.

I had 'lost' my producer for a minute and had nobody else to help me. This prompted me to grab Top 40 instrumental rap tracks and create my own remixes and my own songs to already existing music. When I had burnt about two hundred copies of my mixtapes, I started handing them out in my neighbourhood, sometimes even through the McDonald's drive through. With each copy that was downloaded, I felt a sense of pride and success. Nobody was going to stop me. The mixtape was true and authentic to what Hip-Hop was all about. I rapped about my hardships on the show and the ways in which I would never be hunted or have my music hidden by these people. There wasn't one person who could take my music down again or remove me off any charts because this came from the streets. It was shocking, almost a malfeasance to the whole music industry. But there was nothing anybody could do about it. I was getting my name out there and I didn't care if people didn't like it.

I knew my mountainous pilgrimage had only really just begun, but when a car pulled up outside of my house one day playing one of the tracks from my mixtape, I knew my climb also wasn't near finished... I ran outside, assuming it was a friend who had come to visit and who was playing the mixtape. It wasn't... It was a complete stranger who was stopped at the traffic lights in a 4WD, bopping his head to my remix of a Drake song.

It was at that moment that I knew I was onto something. I knew if only I had the opportunity to do so, I could inspire and touch people. I ran inside to start on my second mixtape right away. As I opened my computer, an email from Star Power's mother company alerted my attention. I clicked the cursor to open it and was confused when I saw the email's subject.

STAR POWER SEARCH UK

UK? As in United Kingdom?

Chapter Eighteen

Ten Thousand Miles Forward, Ten Thousand Miles Back

In our minds we reach certain goals only to have them replaced by new ones. Where once possessing one apple was enough, once you've acquired one apple that no longer satisfies you; the need for more converts to the need for two. This converts to five. Then, the whole fruit basket becomes crucial to you, and before you know it you need the whole fruit store.

At some point, it became part of my daily regime to look back on my career and study myself. I would ask myself questions like: *Where am I? Where will I be in 20 years? Where will I be in one year? What will I have accomplished by the time I 'grow up'?*

These questions were a form of depression; my emotions were an explosive ticking bomb ready to explode like Hiroshima. In my mind I was nothing. I hadn't accomplished anything and I was nothing special. Comparing myself to others was a terrible, nefarious habit that I had picked up, and it was especially difficult whenever I saw the show or an ad for the next season. If a rival competitor booked a magazine interview and I didn't, I thought it meant that I was failing. To me it didn't matter that I was recording or releasing music, I had to do what they were doing too or else I felt inadequate. Fear of being insufficient took a hold of me and I had to do everything possible to allay this feeling. Of course, intellectually, I knew that I was doing whatever was in my power to move forward, but my emotions told me that this wasn't enough.

*

When I finally comprehended what the email had said, I couldn't believe what I was reading. Star Power auditions had already begun again in Australia and I knew that I might have had another opportunity to try out again. Why did I want to put myself through that again? I didn't know. All I knew was that I felt as if having been eliminated from the show was an injustice and a wrongdoing that needed to be corrected. I needed closure and I needed to prove that I was right about myself and to show the producers that they had made a mistake. As an adult now, I realise that sometimes nobody cares if you're right or wrong. The harsh reality is that they don't care at all. Having me go back on their show to 'prove' myself would have been a laughable concept to these people. They didn't care about feelings or second chances, which is why the email shocked my anatomy in more ways than one.

Dear NOA,

It read...

Whilst your place on the Australian Star Power was short lived, we would love to offer you an opportunity to participate in the UK Star Power search this April. Please inform us if you are interested. Unfortunately, due to strict budget restrictions, we will be unable to fund your trip, however, if you would like to make the trek to London we would be more than happy to accommodate a private meeting between you and our producers here.

Kindest regards,

The Music Company.

I was sceptical about the whole offer because they were asking for me to pay for my own trip. A company like that obviously had enough money to send me over, but other than a passing moment of cynicism, I didn't really think anything more of it at the time. I had two weeks to get there and I packed my bags immediately. I didn't have enough money for the trip, but my mother borrowed some money from my grandmother to help pay for it. Going to London on my own was going to be a great personal challenge, but it was something that I felt I had to do. It felt like I was in one of those movies where the struggling artists find themselves moving overseas to get their big break at an audition. I really felt that the hero of this movie, the underdog succeeding, could be me. With my gloves, beanie and scarf on ready for the London weather, I gripped onto the handle of my oversized suitcase full of NOA outfits and took one of the most gigantic leaps of faith a nineteen year old could make.

Goodbye family. Hello London.

*

I've always gone to great lengths to get what I want, whether I do so through the use of guilt-trip tactics, guerrilla warfare or simply with a charming smile; I've always had the gift of perseverance. My earliest memory of this that I can recall is the story of a discarded old doll named Jemima.

While most of the public will assume that singers are in the industry for fame and fortune, that isn't always the case. Yes, a nicer car and a nicer house could be a lovely, almost marvellous thing. However, I don't believe I was born to become some sort of money snatching musician. My quest has always been to open the minds and opinions of the public about acceptance and social change. Not everything is black and white. This is something I had to explain to my whole family with Jemima.

I was about three or four, before dancing and playing with dolls became a forbidden activity. My family and I were over at my Aunty Kathy's house and my sister and I were playing house with my two cousins. The surroundings of this memory have blurred over the years, but I remember my grandfather being there and giving my sister and my two cousins new Barbie dolls. I, of course, did not get a doll; I got Pokémon cards. We all jumped with excitement and, while I was upset that I didn't get a Barbie doll, I was just as happy to have received my favourite video game cards.

Thinking back now, I realise that the encounter I'm about to mention has, in a way, shaped my life. As we were leaving to go home from the family gathering, I noticed a plastic-faced ragdoll. It had curly brown hair tied up in a ponytail and was lying in a pot plant outside the front door on the veranda. The doll was soiled and as black as soot and its body was mangled as if it had been thrown and left there carelessly a long time ago. *Here was my chance to get what I wanted...*

"Mama, look at the poor dolly, she needs a hospital!" I yelled as I ran to grab the doll, brushing the dirt gently out of its hair.

"Don't touch it, you'll get your hands dirty, leave it!" My mother demanded, and she grabbed my arm and began wiping away the mud from my hands.

"No Mum, listen... I need to save her, she's going to die... She... she doesn't... know how to live outside..." I muttered, desperately holding back tears.

I knew exactly what I was doing, even at four years old. I knew the act was cute and would most likely get me what I wanted, and I knew I didn't want to be left out, the only one without a doll. I wanted a doll to play with too. Not only that, this was the first lesson I received in regards to helping others. The doll was broken and had no home. The girls had abandoned her in preference for their new Barbie dolls. It wasn't fair and I understood the unfairness of the doll's predicament. It wasn't her fault that a brighter, skinnier, shinier and more plastic version of a doll was replacing the girls' perfectly decent rag doll. Did she not still have exactly the same role to play in their lives as the Barbie? Wasn't she still able to bring happiness and imagination to playing? Well, yes, she was. Then why had she been left in a pot plant while Barbie got to sit up in the tree house?

It was a combination of acting and a real understanding for loss that made me beg to save and to keep Jemima. Because my parents were ready to leave, they reluctantly agreed to let me keep Jemima and care for her at home. It's quite funny now that I think of it, because years later my father decided to throw away my entire doll collection and the only doll he missed was Jemima. She and I were meant to be. I was obsessed with 'saving' dolls from that point forward and would only buy dolls at the shops that had missing parts. Of course that made it easier on my mother's wallet because most of these were sale items or had been reduced due to damages. For me though, it was a valiant act of protection and redemption. I did this up until my father's 'destroy the dolls day', and it was that day that changed my role as a doll owner to that of a fashion designer and seamstress for my sister's dolls.

On my sixteenth birthday, I actually re-bought all of the dolls (mainly Sailor Moon dolls) that my father had thrown away in his rampage. Nothing ever stops me when I want something. It could be years later, but I will remain strong... waiting for the right moment to come back and prove you wrong. There was nothing wrong with me wanting a doll. Despite what my father might think, dolls don't define a person's sexuality. It was my father's biggest fear that my interaction with anything feminine would mean that I would grow up gay. But I wasn't buying it, not even at four years of age! My little 'saviour' story was only a ploy to get what I wanted and, as I got older, that particular trick didn't work anymore. That didn't mean that I stopped getting what I wanted though. I waited until I knew there was nothing my father could do about it and then proved him wrong.

*

I felt like I was proving the Australian Star Power wrong by going to London. Star Power London's credibility had way more value in the industry than the Australian show had. Huge bands and solo artists had made an immense worldwide impact coming from the London show, with our home-grown Australian winners never making it overseas with any song. It felt like participating in the same program and auditioning for a bigger format this time, was the best payback possible. The Australian show had already started to audition for the next year's series and I hadn't been called back at all. Many contestants who don't make it through in one year, get a call back to try again the following year. Nobody called me and nobody emailed. Getting the London offer was a bigger and better opportunity. I was definitely going to prove the Australian producers wrong. They had made a stupid decision in letting me go because I am the type of person who never quits!

*

My trip to London was extraordinary. While I had no idea where I was or where I was going half of the time, it was an amazing chance to be totally independent and explore a country that had so much history to it. I made sure I was there a couple of days extra to visit the national treasures like the Big Ben, the London Eye, London Bridge and the Tower of London. But the most important place for me was Warner Brother's Studios where Harry Potter had been created and filmed. I have always loved Bellatrix and Voldemort. To be completely honest, I almost wanted Voldemort to win those mighty battles as I was reading the Harry Potter books. Perhaps that's the Villain in me! I was also lucky enough to have had distant relatives who lived just outside the heart of London city, who were kind enough to show me around town and take me out to fun places. I was only with them for the last two days of my trip.

I had no idea how to get to the meeting at the Star Power office. With a couple of stops on the London tube, I ended up finding the building of the UK Star Power offices and made my way up to the top floor for the meeting. I was dressed in NOA's Sunday best, which meant my matching sequined tracksuit was on and my bleach blonde hair was in a neat Samurai bun. As the elevator door opened, I noticed a congregation of people waiting in seats outside a large black door. There were about forty people in front of me. I sat in line and began a conversation with a lady next to me. I don't remember her name, but we'll call her Toya.

Toya was twenty-seven years old and had a son who was nine. She was a lovely lady with a generous heart. She had quit her job to follow her dream of becoming a singer and was also there ready for a meeting with the producers. This is where I realised that the forty odd people in the room were all there to have a meeting with

Star Power UK's producers. This wasn't a private meeting, it was a bloody casting call! I started eavesdropping and I overheard a few girls say their managers had set this meeting up for them.

Here we go again!

They had called and collected acts that they were already interested in and wanted to meet with in real life, to see if they were TV worthy. These meetings took about ten minutes each, so naturally, with forty people in front of me, I waited about six hours. Toya thought I was crazy for dropping everything, with such late notice, to travel halfway around the world just for this one ten minute meeting. I thought Toya was crazy for quitting her job to try pursue singing as a full-time career. While I've always believed performing has been my true calling, I'm not an idiot. Singing doesn't pay the bills when you're starting out. If anything, you need to be earning other money to enable you to put your own records out there. How do you get that money to promote your music? You need to work.

When they called Toya's name, I moved into the next available seat, waiting for my turn to finally come. My nerves were a little rattled, but I mentally prepared like any other audition. This wasn't an exclusive personal meeting, it was very definitely just another audition; I had to make sure I stood out.

When Toya came out of the room and I saw tears start to well in her eyes, I asked her what was wrong.

"They said no! How am I going to make ends meet?" she gathered her hands at her face and ran to the bathroom, white as a ghost.

Her situation was horrific. Sure, I've felt rejection before, but to rely on this business to raise your child? It's a very hard and almost impossible thing to do. Perhaps the reason I will never forget her is not because I felt sorry for her, but because she really had faith that she could bring in money for her boy by using her talent... and boy could she sing!

I entered the room quite with a relentless determination. I was here to win and that's exactly what I was going to do. At a table before me were three individuals, one of whom I recognised from some behind-the-scenes Star Power UK episodes where they took viewers backstage to discover behind the scenes' 'secrets' after the show's episode finished airing. He had a direct connection to Sal Horse, who was the CEO and head of every single Star Power show around the world and who had huge broadcast connections with major companies and record labels, like the company in Australia who owned most of the country's national press coverage.

Sal was a public figure who was known for connecting himself with the largest networks that each country possessed and signing agreements with them to broadcast Star Power and gain earnings from every contestant that the shows produced. Because these huge networks and companies want in on the cash, they agree to air the show on their channels and promote it in every way they can; hence the huge company in Australia who agreed to do the same with the Star Power Australia winners. The more money Sal made, the more money the networks made in return. It was a percentage-based system that both parties were happy to agree to. Even though Sal wasn't there, his stand-in was still just as scary as he would have been. The other two people were camera crew. All that was left for me to do was sing.

I was asked the same questions that Star Power Australia had asked me at my first audition in Sydney. It was the same thing all over again, except this show would be broadcast in front of the whole of the UK, which is about three times Australia's population. More people would see this show! More people would become fans. It was a platform that was way bigger than the Australian show's little podium.

This guy didn't look at me once.

"I'll be singing 'When Angels Cry' by The Duke." I said to the top of his head. It was the same routine as before, and the same song I had auditioned with in Sydney.

"Go, on then," he uttered.

The British have a very abrupt way of speaking, so I didn't know whether he was being rude and already hated me or whether he was just doing his job.

He was quite elfish in appearance, but had a really powerful look on his face. This guy had some serious power around here. His posture was really straight and the way he carried himself seemed as if he had a lot of influence.

He still didn't look up, but waited for me to begin to sing.

I started shaky, my nerves got to me a little, but I finished with my rap, nice and strong, and held a high note right at the end.

"Thank you, we'll be in touch... NEXT!"

That was it! That's all I got.

I had travelled around the globe to hear less than ten words from this dude's mouth.

I wasn't really sure what to do at that point. I didn't know whether to walk out of the office or if there was more to the story. I stumbled my way out trying to figure out what was going on. As I exited the room, a lady I hadn't noticed on my way in handed me a sheet of paper which explained that I would be contacted in two weeks with a result.

I stayed in London for the next two weeks until I was on my last dollar. For breakfast I was eating £2 bagels from the nearby deli. I had explained my situation to the hotel manager, who kindly allowed me to stay in my room, free of charge, for an extra week. A place of hope and determination became a place of curiosity and waiting. The cobblestone streets I walked on everyday are something I will never forget. They taught me that with every negative experience in life comes refurbishment. While you may feel like you've fallen or gone backwards, there will always be an opportunity to rectify your actions or the result of someone else's actions. I had my dolls safe and sound, bought again and secure in their mint condition boxes. Whatever happened with Star Power UK didn't matter anymore. Of course I wanted to be on the show more than anything else in the world, but as the days ticked past I just kept convincing myself that even if I received a 'no', I would have another chance somewhere down the track to get prove them wrong. If I could wait over ten years for my dolls, then I could wait a hundred years for a chance to sing to the masses again. But I knew that this was where I belonged... in front of huge audiences.

I had waited with so much angst to prove that Star Power Australia had been wrong about letting me go. Just like getting Jemima, I wasn't going to quit on this mission to get what I wanted. By the end of that two weeks, with no more information from Star Power UK, I flew back home.

Chapter Nineteen

Mob Ties

In the mob you're taught to be loyal at all costs and that being an informant is the lowest form of betrayal and makes you a rat. A rat is a rat: the lowest of the low, and you keep away from rats. You don't go near them, you don't smell them, and you don't associate with any of them. A rat is seen as the lowest form of scum in society. A rat is somebody who snitches on others and participates in the dirtiest of dirty crimes with little regard for their family, who are often put in harm's way. Don't get me wrong, the mob is filled with unscrupulous criminals, but a true gangster does not involve their families in their wrongdoings. Rats only look out for themselves, they leave a bad smell behind in their wake, along with leaving the innocent with more problems than they started out with.

*

You can't trust anybody is this industry. That's a sad, but true fact. Everybody has their own agenda and every single rising star will just as soon stab you in the back to get to the top. They will do anything to be that star they've always thought they were. This is what I call a sell-out; this is something I will never be. Nor will I ever play or create music that I don't love or that I feel no connection to.

While I was working on my own material and releasing my music independently, Natalie, from the group Senses, decided it would be her time to shine and so made plans to audition again for Star Power Australia. Natalie and her friend, Jackie, another former Star Power contestant, had both decided to audition. Just a couple of months after I returned from London, I agreed to go with them to also try my luck again. For me, it felt kind of like the last shot I had left to make an impact, with the help of television, in Australia.

I had never liked Jackie. I thought she was a bad influence on Natalie. I knew Jackie before we auditioned for the last Star Power season, and yet she pretended like she didn't know me. We even went to university together, but if that's how she wanted to leave things, then that was fine by me! Karma is something that can bite you on the butt when you least expect it, especially when you sell out or become a rat. And karma, I told myself, would come around to visit Jackie.

The same year I went to London, Jackie, after the Star Power finals, went to the US and was signed by a major record label. However, she was dropped a few weeks later with no release and no help because, according to other friends, she had a bad attitude. Acting like you're better than everyone is a disrespectful way to behave, and in this industry, it is like signing your own death sentence. Most of the people you work with in this industry are already more established than you. It's like a mob circle that needs an initiation to get into. You need millions of views on your videos and a large social media following, but, ironically, talent is on the bottom of the list of requirements. Plus, you can use all the help you can get from established artists and industry professionals. Once you're in this mob, you have a name for yourself. Those individuals with a name obviously don't appreciate getting attitude from a bottom-feeder who needs their help, hence Jackie's label drop.

Natalie was fortunate enough, unlike me, to have made it onto the show that next year. She had also dumped the group and played up her storyline of how she'd come back to the show alone, without Senses, to try things as a solo artist. For me, this was one of the biggest sell-outs I had ever seen. You don't dump your group, leaving them to die, and then head into the spotlight by yourself; but really, I shouldn't judge, I have no idea what agreement the Sense's group members had made with one another.

Natalie went on as a solo artist, and I promoted her on all forms of social media since, at that time, my following as a solo artist had surpassed her group and her own individual social media pages. While I sat hustling and busting my behind doing things alone, the support I gave to Natalie was not reciprocated. Her status began to elevate, whereas mine remained the same. Jackie had a bigger social media following than both of us, having been a finalist in the year that we had all competed and I had been cut for 'knowing too much'. Naturally, Natalie and Jackie used each other in the most pretentious and counterfeit ways possible in order to gain a larger public following for themselves. I found the whole thing upsetting as I had been a great friend to Natalie and we had opened up to each other about our families and our partners... as friends do. I had even taken her shopping to buy her clothes for her new solo debut because her style, in my view, was mediocre and I thought my help could assist her in creating a better image and brand, fashion-wise. These things I did because I felt that, if it wasn't me who made it, at least one of us from our hometown could show Australia what we could do, despite not coming from an affluent area. I had even gone to watch her perform, while Jackie at this point, angry and jealous, was nowhere to be seen. It was when she sold out completely to the show that my friendship with Natalie turned for the worst. I didn't want to surround myself with cop-outs. Be real or don't be at all—it was as simple as that.

*

Any rat in a picture dictionary should have my father's face plastered all over it… in bold! We grew up with money. Not plenty, but enough to get whatever we wanted. My sister and I always had the latest Play Stations, Gameboys, trampolines and more. My mother was always fighting with my father and, of the many conversations they shared, I would always hear: *Where did that money come from?*

I wondered this myself and, as I got older, more and as more things became clearer to me. Through conversations with other family members, I discovered that my father had been in jail at some point during my first year of life. I can't vouch for the legitimacy of these tales as they were stories only told to me by others, and not my immediate family as these kinds of discussions are taboo in an ethnic home. You don't talk about money, jail or sex in front of your parents, aunts and uncles or grandparents.

The first time I noticed my father was up to no good was a night I was awoken by my parents yelling about a woman named Paula. Paula was my father's mistress; in most European cultures a mistress is called a *Pouta*. So once I heard about Paula, I named her Paula the *Pouta*. Cheating is something that I've never understood. If you want to cheat or are unhappy with your relationship or marriage, tell your partner first. I didn't necessarily have any hate towards Paula, how could I—I was unaware what knowledge she possessed about my mother and my family. It's not a woman's fault if they fall in love with a man who perhaps tells them that he is single. That was probably the first rat-like manoeuvre I discovered that my father had committed.

As I grew up, family members closer to my age revealed more stories to me about my father and his brothers. According to them, the three brothers owned a car depository for used cars that needed repairs. The brothers would acquire these damaged or in-need-of-repair cars and sell them privately for large sums of money. Most of the time, these cars were not actually fixed, rather a bandage of some sort was placed on top of a problem so that buyers wouldn't find out the cars' real issues. As the years went on, the brothers all specialised in a specific field: one brother dealt with the electrical side of cars, the other dealt with the vehicles' exteriors. My father dealt with engines. They were a fairly well-known workshop in the late eighties and early nineties and began to bring in lots of business and lots of money.

Now this wouldn't have been information that shocked anybody, so these family members would not have told me anything had there not been more to the story. According to these family members, cars would be stolen or acquired in many illegal ways and then resold privately by the brothers to make extra money on the side. Their legitimate business was just a façade for what was really going on at the car depository.

When my father went to jail, one of his brothers coerced the third brother into selling the workshop because they were beginning to be investigated by the federal police. They split the money they had in a shared bank account between the two of them and left my father penniless. I guess being a rat ran in the family, as they say: *Monkey see, monkey do.*

When my father got out of jail, we were left with nothing and my parents struggled financially for many long years. This was another reason why I felt like it was my responsibility to get my sister and myself out of the hole created by my parents. My father was not only a fraud, but was also a wife-beating cheat.

Towards the end of my teenage life, whilst moving out of our family home when my parents finally divorced, I also found abortion papers. My mother had fallen whilst pregnant when I was about fifteen years old and my father, not wanting another child, threatened to kill the both of them if she had the baby. Sometimes I struggle to find a clear reason why my sister and I were spared this Hunger Games' experience, but then I remember how I almost didn't make it. My unborn twin died from my father's abuse, just not in quite the same way as this particular baby. *Why did he end up keeping my sister and me then?* To be honest, I don't think he actually wanted me... I was just the accidental survivor. Perhaps he *had* meant to kill both of us? Either way, in my eyes, he will forever be a rat.

*

As Natalie progressed on the show, she sold-out completely when she agreed to join a group created by the show to imitate another girl band that was hugely successful in the UK at the time. That's all these shows ever try to do: imitate what's already hot overseas in hope the same formula will work here in Australia. Some-times it does work, I mean, Serenity Hayes became a Britney Spears equivalent and, a few years prior, there had been a Jason Derulo look-alike who came out of another singing show and who is also still quite successful in Sydney. So, in the show's true nature, Natalie was placed in a new girl group, her solo career ending as quickly as it started. This was ironic, as she had dumped her own girl group only to be placed in another. In my eyes, I could see this was not what she wanted, and I wondered why she would agree to what could only be a backwards step.

I think that idea of fame and glory gets infused into people's head. I had been in the industry since I was very little, so I felt kind of immune to these notions as wants. Fame and glory doesn't simply land on people, they are just some of the benefits that come with hard work. Without staying true to who you are and working hard, fame and glory vanishes quite quickly. In addition, it's not fame and followers that define you. It's the music you sing and the music and visuals you produce that express who you are. I could never agree to do something just for the sake of being successful.

In the end we all make mistakes. I had learnt from my mistakes quite young and perhaps this was Natalie's time to learn. The created girl group that she found herself in only made it through a few rounds of the live shows before getting the axe. They disbanded a few weeks later due to creative differences, which in this world means that all the girls in the group probably wanted to sing lead. It was at this point that Natalie realised that everything in this industry was not as it seemed... and our friendship went back to normal. It was easy to forgive her because I always felt her intentions were in the right place. It's easy to get caught up in this industry and I do believe that some people who do so are genuinely sorry in the end or they become people that aren't really who they are on the inside. Either way, you change, for the better or worse.

During this time, I was asked by a sister label to come to a meeting with one of the main record labels affiliated with Star Power and the network that the show was on. They had asked me to create and establish a boy band that was made up of 'three types of NOAs. I believe they saw the potential in Natalie's group, but also saw how catty young girls can be in regards to jealousy and wanting the spotlight. Thus, a boy band, made to mimic the success of a very famous band in Asia that consisted of quirky pop singer's like me, would be their next attempt.

What makes me a stand-alone artist is the fact that I don't need a rapper or dancer to form a group. I have all these skills myself and use them in my solo performances. These groups all consist of individuals who are strong at only one particular form of performance. I may not have been a Hercules at everything, but I could most definitely, with my own hands, put on a show that encompassed everything that these performers did singularly. This was why I politely declined the label's offer. In paraphrased words, they basically told me that if I didn't comply with their request, I wouldn't ever be back on the show. I was aware that their power of authority was quite minimal and the threat was quite empty, but I knew that their statement was true: my time was up on Star Power and there was no going back to it. I had released too much music on my own and my music spoke to them in a language that they didn't understand. I was a fighter and would never agree to anything that I didn't believe in and thus, I would always be a problem to them: somebody who didn't listen to them and didn't obey the rules.

*

There's a hierarchy in the mob as well. While my father was king in his version of the mob, in the larger scheme of things he was not a man of any status whatsoever. To be undermined by his brothers without a word was what made him pathetic. He couldn't stick up for himself, even if he wanted to. It was his older brother who called all the shots. They had apprentices and quite a lot of other people involved in this car ring. My godfather owned a large liquor business in Australia and, as far as I know, he also held a great role in covering up whatever these men were up to. Presumably this is all in the past, but the last time I saw my father, he had just purchased a large workshop, this time alone, so who knows. There was one room joined to this workshop that had one desk with two chairs on opposite sides of it; a 'business' desk no doubt.

Monsters become monsters only because of the monsters they have seen before them. My father's older brother was also a wife-beating rat and, according to my father, my grandfather held similar qualities (not that this was ever revealed to his grandchildren).

This time had been horrible for my mother too. She was forbidden to study again and was unable to acquire a good job to provide for us. Back in the early days when we didn't need that second income, she had left her career in pathology to raise me. After my father's stint in jail, she was forced to become a sandwich hand as too much time passed in the medical field for her to re-enter without taking more study and passing additional exams. My father's disapproval of her

continuing her studies, left her stuck working in the take away food industry for over twenty years... just to feed us. I guess this is where my determination comes from. My mother never let us go hungry and did everything she could to buy us what we needed and wanted. I don't have any children of my own, but I do think that I would kill for my child if I had to. In fact, I see most of my friends as my children, (I'm the one everyone usually comes to for advice) and I know that I have done some pretty dangerous things for them to keep them protected and safe.
*

My third mixtape was not as successful as my other two, but ended up being the last release I gave my audience for quite some time. At this time, I was very disheartened and Natalie's inside scoop on what was happening on the show made me just as upset as I had been the last time I heard about the show's debaucheries. My producer at this time was stuck in another country waiting for his American Visa to be approved and I felt stranded by everybody, in a musical sense. Most producers were working with winners like Serenity Hayes or people with large social media followings, like Jackie. I was stuck by myself trying to do everything alone. I found that everything that I usually did with the help of others was taking me such a long time, and everything became a huge effort to do by myself.

But as usual, nothing was going to stop me.

Chapter Twenty

Giving Up is Hard to Do

While I try to be hopeful, I have always been somewhat pessimistic in my attitude towards certain situations. I hope and dream that things will turn out the way I want and for the best, but I'm always aware of reality. I prepare myself for the absolute worst, so that any positive progression becomes something I truly appreciate. I'm a realist. I understand probability and the way that humans interact with one another. Chance does not simply fall into your hands without you trying to catch it. It's like playing the lottery: chances are you're not going to win. You hope for a windfall, but deep down inside you know that you wasted your ticket purchase on the slim hope that your life could change. You may try your hardest to secure the best possible outcome; you may think that perhaps a maths calculation or a specific newsagency location will give you the upper hand in delivering you a win. While you may try your absolute best to select the right numbers, there's really nothing you can do to change the outcome, other than buy a ticket and hope. I'm a fan of hope, I support hope, but only if you're aware that the desired outcome is mostly illusory.

*

As well as our basic instinct to survive, we have inherent instincts to succeed and to not be embarrassed. We are taught that failure means the opposite of succeeding, it means we will, thereafter, become an embarrassment in the eyes of all those who thought we would triumph. And with failure, comes shame.

"It's a shame you didn't get further…"

"Oh, what a loser, no wonder he didn't make it…"

"Give it up already…"

"I wish he had made it…"

I had failed. I had been eliminated, and it didn't matter who made the commentary that went along with the aftermath of my trials. All the comments reflected people who either felt sorry for me, or saw me as a pathetic and public failure. I find it a funny concept that when you are at your peak and at your most successful, everybody wants to be your best friend. They will call you successful and praise your accomplishments to the lofty heights. But the moment you stumble and fall, they distance themselves like you are diseased; they are ashamed of you, embarrassed by your failure. There are also a handful of people who believe and support somebody so much that their hearts break at the idea that their beloved had, in fact, failed. They feel so much sadness and sorrow. In my eyes, both groups of people are as bad as each other. One group of people are feeble and fake and will support you like a yo-yo, these are your good-time supporters. The others, will feel so much sorrow for you that they'll tiptoe around your failure in hope of not contributing to any further hurt. The good-time supporters and the heartbreakers; nobody is real. At this point in time, I found myself either surrounded with or abandoned by all these types of people.

It's hard to keep a positive outlook on things that aren't doing so well. Sure, I felt as though I had conquered the music scene in Australia with something different and innovative, but there was no true recognition available to me. I was wearing myself out and working myself to the bone to produce my music alone, but it seemed to me that the more I created, the less people cared about what I was releasing. It felt like all my hard work and effort was for nothing. It became almost ignominious for me to continue and I found it harder and harder to find the drive to do so.

After two years had passed since being on the show, I had been totally forgotten by the Australian public. I felt worn out, betrayed even. Those who knew me, now saw me as a failure and those who tried their best to continue to follow my career, slowly turned away to follow the rest of the crowd. How can you follow or support something that no one else is embracing? Why listen to NOA when Rihanna just released a new single? It's social suicide to be different and nobody wanted to take that risk anymore. I was competing with something I couldn't compete with any longer. I wondered if I even wanted to take the risks myself anymore, if it was worth pushing myself to improve, to perform, to produce if I was never going to win. No one was listening to me and I couldn't beat what was already out there. There was even a point where I thought my music was too ahead of its time. One of my records had incorporated Arabian drums and a mandolin, both sounds blending to become something melodious, but innovative. Guess who cared? Nobody. But when Jason Derulo released one of his songs a year later that incorporated the same sounds, he found himself at the top of his musical career. Everybody loved him. I did feel betrayed by the public and angry that there was no acknowledgement that I was doing new and interesting things.

*

I always hoped, dreamed I guess, from quite a young age, that things would go favourably regarding my career. I remember watching newly released music videos from the US, studying them for that secret ingredient. I would stay up until all hours of the night as their time difference clashed with ours. I would stay awake until four or five in the morning waiting for a new music video or a new song to be dropped, wishing, yearning, that one-day people would do the same for me.

There was even one point where I would disrupt my sleeping patterns to practise what it would feel like to be travelling around the world, on tour, with no sleep and with so much to do. I would set my alarm for one in the morning and force myself to stay awake until the following night, then I would only allocate two hours of sleep the following night. In my head, because I hoped so much that I was going to make it, I needed to be prepared for that outcome. I needed to be ready, and this was my training.

Books were also a favourite pastime of mine. I would buy biographies of all my favourite singers and read about their path to success: how they got there, what moves they made, how they lost their fame. I studied their successes. I studied their failures. I was desperate to learn their secrets, their tricks. I needed to know what to do and what not to do. I watched as Madonna crassly tore up interview questions because she felt that a statement needed to be made about interviews and reporters. I analysed how Michael Jackson had managed to remain so influential for so long. His iconic dance moves strategically created so that people would be performing the same move every time they heard his songs.

I worked so very hard, from such a young age, to do my best to support the idea that I was going to be a star. While I knew the chances of that happening were one in a million, I still hoped, till the very end, that the little boy who had danced and sang and created fashion statements would fulfil his dream of success. I remember even doing the maths when I was younger, calculating just what it would take to be a star. If there were seven billion people in the world, and one in a million make it to stardom, then there would be seven thousand people who succeed. In my mind, my chances got a little bit higher just knowing that.

*

Sammy had set up a meeting for me with a man, Bernard, whose status in the music industry was an important one. Bernard was, I recall, a manager or producer who had been working for a major record label for quite a while. Sammy had asked Bernard to meet with me to give me some advice about the direction my music was going. I was excited to meet with him because somebody with first-hand experience usually has the best advice. In addition, most industry executives have large networks and connections. If he liked what he saw, there was a high chance that he would tell other important people about who I was and what I was trying to achieve. Hearing that Bernard may be able to help me, I made sure I looked the part and spoke very nicely. Unfortunately, our conversation lasted about five minutes because the man was busy and needed to attend to his own matters. He had told me that my music videos were cheap and that the only way I was going to make it was to jack up the femininity and play the 'I'm a unicorn' card with a bigger budget. Because of the success my R&B mixtape had, I had asked him what the chances were of me pursuing R&B. His response was, "If you ever try to do anything other than Lady Gaga pop, your career will be over as fast as it started."

This made me mad. He hadn't even heard my mixtape, but was making a judgement based only on my appearance. In his eyes, my videos were cheap and tasteless, but in my eyes, I had poured my heart and soul into them, they were gold. Labels spend hundreds and thousands of dollars on videos that looked a whole lot tackier than mine. I did what I could with what I had. The more people tell me I can't do something, the more I get the urge to make sure I prove them wrong. He looked at me as though I was the dirt on his shoes. As my mind began analysing all the hard work I had achieved, he brought me back to reality with his arrogance.

"Are you listening to anything I've told you? Don't waste my time. If you ever try to do anything other than Lady Gaga pop, your career will be over as fast as it started, do you understand?" He got up to leave without as much as a handshake, and I just let him go, too annoyed to try to turn the meeting around, too angry to try to find any useful insight from what he had said. You can't teach an old dog new tricks, just like you can't teach people who are set in their ways to be open minded.

While Sammy was still preoccupied with settling into the US, I decided I would take matters into my own hands. I was going to write, produce and release an R&B song from scratch. I was going to hire an awesome videographer and change my look completely. Screw the opinions of all of these people! If I was going to be a failure, I wanted to fail spectacularly while trying my hardest, I wanted to be a failure who did anything in their power to succeed before the fall.

I'm a villain. I don't play by the rules of others. I make my own rules.

I grew a beard and took on a stereotypical male rapper look for my next music video. It was called 'In Bed With A Boss' and the video was full of metaphors and allusions about the music industry and the corruption therein. I paired this with a second song called 'Devils Don't Come Home' which saw me in the most feminine outfit I had ever worn. I wanted to present these two seemingly contradictory images just to prove to people that I could morph, that I was not one thing, that I could not be pushed into a pigeon hole. The two songs were a metaphoric story of my journey. The first delved into themes of betrayal, harassment and a hope for change; the second was about revenge, power and anger. I was making visuals and music that told powerful stories. These music videos both told part of an epic story that made me proud.

It was about this time that I exhausted not just myself physically, but all of my resources too. I had no money left and nothing more to give. I was pushing myself physically and emotionally to keep down two part-time jobs; they were cash money jobs and didn't pay very well. How long did I think I was I going to keep this up? What about my future? How was I going to buy a house? Support a future family? On top of that, I had almost finished my university degree, but had delayed my graduation again and again due to all of the other musical projects that I had been involved in. I was exhausted from all of the commitments I had and all of the things I was trying to do to progress my musical career. I was running on empty and was so very, very tired. It was time to face reality and realise that music had to become a hobby rather than a career. It scared me even to think that because I knew I was lying to myself. Music could never be a hobby to me. I hate the word hobby. It's so inconsistent and it has no bearing upon the depth of passion I have toward music.

But I had no choice. Facts are facts. Music wasn't making me any money. I was spending thousands and thousands of dollars and getting nothing in return. No revenue, no new followers, no progress. How much longer was I going to entertain this selfish desire for more? I had to face reality. I needed to rest, to recoup and to gather myself again. I would have to sit back and rely on chance.

*

During this period I decided to get a full-time job managing a bowling alley near my house. I needed the money; I needed to be 'responsible'. This meant managing staff, cleaning balls and shoes and watching people bowl down wooden lanes, taking out their frustrations on white pins by throwing a bowling ball angrily and unnecessarily like the Hulk. *Fun!*

Work soon became tedious, the same thing every day. I was getting paid well, but I was making all this money every day for somebody else. I couldn't quite comprehend this idea at all. It made me frustrated that I knew that I was worth more than what I was doing; it broke my heart to know what I was letting go of to keep this mindless job just so that I could help make ends meet for my family.

I'm not saying that I had given up exactly, because I don't think I would ever be capable of doing such a thing, but I was so tired and I know I needed to accept the notion that, for a while at least, this was going to be my life. It was a depressing realisation, one that saw me retreating from myself and from my dream so that my mind became numbed and dull. I was still dabbling in music, but my lack of general inspiration in life had left me at a writer's block. I wasn't a happy person and my song writing became terrible, reflecting my depressed inner world.

The idea of a 'real' or 'normal' life has always scared me. I'm just not cut out to be a nine to five worker. I can't do the same thing every day without any self-benefit other than a pitiful amount of money. I don't see the point and it kind of hurt me somehow. I became very depressed, sluggish. I had lost motivation completely; I had lost the desire to interact with life. Since letting go of ferociously chasing my dreams and taking this job, although I had made a great group of friends at work that made my life bearable, somewhere along the way I had lost myself. Passion had left me, there was no use for him anymore, and hope had left me alone. Is this what it felt like to be a 'normal' civilian? Secretly, I cried to myself... This was not how my story was supposed to end.

*

Wanting something so bad can be a frightening experience. I had wanted a music career so desperately that I had almost destroyed myself in the process. People pass away all the time and this is immensely sad, but it's dangerous for someone alive to think that they can resurrect the dead. It's an impossible wish. At some point you have to come to terms with the death. My life had felt like trying to resurrect the dead.

I have always wanted to change the world and make our social connections as humans easier and more honest than they are. Some people say that to dream to change the world or make it a better place is a foolish wish. But my heart disagrees.

Music has always been there for me, in times of fear and sadness and joy. Music has been there from the beginning of time. It has been used to communicate, to mourn, celebrate, teach and commemorate. I never planned on giving up on my dream. But what was I supposed to do? What was I meant to do when I could no longer see a way forward, when I barely had the strength to maintain the barest semblance of life? I still held my dream deep, deep inside me, I hadn't given up on my dream, but if felt like my dream had given up on me. What could I do now?

All of my friends and family supported me through my sadness. They knew I was hurting and rallied around to help me heal. I guess they hoped that, in time, I would fully come to terms with my 'new' life, that I would regain my old enthusiasm, my humour, my love and that I would laugh with them again.

But this was a deep sadness at the core of my very being and, as I expected, it would not go away...

Chapter Twenty-One

Time for Redemption

It's very rare that we get second chances. They are as uncommon as red diamonds.

Some opportunities are those one in a million that they talk about, that golden ticket, that lottery win, that wheel of fortune. You're lucky if you get just one of these chances, but who would get two?

*

The bowling alley was empty as I grabbed my bag to close up. The bowling balls had been placed neatly next to one another and the service counter was impeccably clean. Everything seemed neat and tidy, ready for tomorrow, and my day's work was finally over. Like every other night, I switched off the lights, checked all the emergency exits and went to alarm the premises.

BEEP... BEEP...

My pocket buzzed and a familiar sound echoed, louder than normal in the silence of the empty bowling lanes.

I took my phone out of my pocket while fumbling for the keys to the alley with my other hand. I opened the email and it read:

Dear NOA,

We would like to invite you to our headquarters regarding your music and your future prospects.

We believe that you will be a fantastic addition to our new music show airing on television next year.

We've seen your work and we love you!

Please reply to this email to confirm your attendance. We look forward to seeing you.

The Music Race

The Music Race was another television program that allowed musicians to sing their own songs and their own original material. The show had been on hiatus after their ratings had dropped and I never thought it would see the light of day again. My heart skipped a beat. I read the email a few times before it actually sunk in. Here was an invitation. Was this my second chance?

I locked and alarmed the bowling alley and got into my car. I looked through the front windscreen and had one thought:

The Villain was back!